I0726223

MAKING MAGIK

A Magik Prep Anthology

AJ Skelly

OTHER WRITING BY AJ SKELLY

The Wolves of Rock Falls Series

First Shift

Rogue Shift

Sworn Shift

Dark Shift

Pack Shift

Lost Shift (coming October 2023)

Magik Prep Academy

Making Magik

Of Flame & Frost (coming March 2023)

Anthologies

Moonlight and Claws

What Darkness Fears

Where Giants Fall

Hidden Villains

Aphotic Love

Fool's Honor

Fantasea

Sharper than Thorns

MAKING MAGIK

A Magik Prep Anthology

AJ Skelly

Quill & Flame
PUBLISHING HOUSE

Copyright © 2023 by AJ Skelly

All rights reserved.

No portion of this book may be reproduced in any form without written permission from the publisher or author, except as permitted by U.S. copyright law.

For my kids.

May you always believe in magic, but may you always know the Truth.

Magik Prep Academy

Magik Prep Academy
An
Egg
&
a
Kiss
AJ Skelly

AN EGG & A KISS

I shove the doors open with a frustrated sigh. First day of my Junior year back at Magik Prep Academy, and the two things I want most are still out of my grasp.

My best friend—the one I've known since kindergarten that morphed into a gorgeous geeky demi-god of a guy two years ago—still has no idea that I've been in love with him since seventh grade. And I still don't have my own dragon egg to hatch.

A piece of silvery-blonde hair falls across my face and I whisk it back behind my ear and sigh wistfully at the scroll feed curling up the wall.

I desperately want to take my heirloom golden quill out of my purse and boldly pen my name on that scroll feed. I've wanted to be a part of the Dragon Hatcher's Apprentice Guild almost as long as I've been in love with Reid. But you have to have your own dragon you've hatched from an egg to be considered. When Mom finally gave her blessing to let me join the Guild, I was overjoyed. I literally did a cartwheel in the living room. Mom's one condition: I had to purchase the egg myself.

Because dragon eggs are prohibitively expensive and Dad's life insurance money is planted firmly in a protected fund that neither Mom nor I can touch until I'm twenty-three, I've been saving since freshman year. And it would have been fine.

Except Mom came down with a nasty case of Sorcerer's Pox. They're not deadly, but they're painful. And the cure, because it's made from the rare black angel hair orchid, is wicked pricey. Mom would have recovered on her own. But it might have been months. I couldn't watch her writhe in silent agony that long, even if she insisted she was fine. Not when I could make all her suffering end with one dose of the cure.

So, I spent my hard-earned dragon egg money. And Mom is fine now, thank the Maker.

Sighing, I absently brush another piece of silvery hair that's fallen in my eyes. Mom still feels guilty that I used my egg money for her cure. She's happy to be well again, but she can't pay me back. And that's okay. I'd rather Mom be healthy. But I'm still disappointed.

I clutch the straps of my bag as I slowly make my way to my locker.

It's still early and I'm not in a rush. The halls slowly fill, the old stones soaking in the noises and releasing some of their age-worn magic into the air. I reach out and twist a string of the iridescent stuff. It shimmers against my pale fingers, and my lips tug into a smile despite my grumpy attitude. Until I see the banner for the Back to School Dance dangling from an arched buttress.

My teeth find my lip as my stomach drops. I want to go with Reid. So much. But I'm afraid I'll ruin everything if I ask him.

I kick the toe of my boot against the flagstone floor. A poof of red magic dusts the tops of my shoes. Orange light shimmers down the hallway, and I know I need to start thinking about getting my things ready for class.

Several people exchange greetings with me as I walk down to my locker. I frown when I realize there's a magiked lock on it. I didn't put it there.

Lifting the lock, my shoulders tense. It's a bio lock. If it's not got my information stored in it and someone put this on here as a prank, I'm going to have to hunt down a janitorial ogre to get it off. And they are *not* morning creatures.

I put my finger on the bottom and feel the quick pull of magic as it springs the mechanism loose, and it drops to my hand. I exhale.

Putting the lock in my purse, the locker door creaks open. And then my mouth hangs loose like a Drop-Jaw waiting for its prey. I blink. I swallow. Quickly I check the locker number.

It's mine.

Nestled there in a soft cloth is the most perfect dragon egg I've ever seen. I'm almost afraid to touch it. It's shiny magenta, speckled with amethyst sparkles.

Reverently, I cup my hands around the precious egg and lift it to my chest. My eyes close as soft warmth and the slight musty scent of *dragon* surround me. I leave my eyes shut until I'm no longer afraid the tears will leak out.

Glancing back into my open locker, there's an envelope. It's thick white parchment with gilt edges. Just seeing it there makes my belly quiver.

Carefully placing the egg back in its soft nest, I nearly cut my finger on the paper as my hands shake trying to open it.

Heat rushes through me when I recognize the writing and tears spring to my eyes again.

Silvey,

I know you've wanted one of these for half of forever. This one is yours. No strings attached. Go put your name on the scroll feed.

But there is one other thing. And I'm writing this so my words don't get all tangled when I try to say them to you.

I smile as I picture how words seem to stick in my friend's mouth when he's frustrated.

My smile fades as I read the last line.

Will you go to the Back to School Dance with me? As my date?

My mouth goes dry and my eyes bulge in their sockets when I read his closing.

Your best friend who would like to explore the possibility of being more,

-Reid

Silvey,

I know you've wanted one of these for half of forever. This one is yours. No strings attached. Go put your name on the scroll feed.

But there is one other thing. And I'm writing this so my words don't get all tangled when I try to say them to you.

Will you go to the Back to School Dance with me?

As my date?

Your best friend who would like to explore the possibility of being more,

-Reid

He's here. He's watching me somewhere. He wouldn't miss seeing my face when I found his gift and read his letter.

Wildly searching the hall, I find a pair of sea-green eyes staring at me from underneath a mop of dark hair. His face is as steady and handsome as ever, but there's a vulnerability there that I've never seen.

Snatching my egg, I dash over to him. Flinging caution to the wind, I leap at him, and plant my lips on his.

Momentarily stunned, he's still as stone for a full second before squeezing me tight.

"Is that a thank-you for the egg or a yes to something else?" he says when we break apart.

"Both," I say with a huge smile.

Sometimes dreams do come true.

Magik Prep Academy

Goggles

AJ Skelly

GOGGLES

I smelled like basilisk poop.

And Tatianna Everblaze was coming toward me with her gaggle of friends.

She was the most beautiful girl at Magik Prep Academy.

Her golden hair was tied back with a red ribbon that matched the occasional flames that rose in her eyes as her inner phoenix flashed. We were seniors this year, but I'd been a goner after the first time we'd had a freshman study session together. Happy fire danced in her eyes as she laughed at something one of the girls said as they neared the basilisk barn.

I groaned. Half my face was still covered by stupid protective goggles. One peek from basilisk eyes and you'd be seeing a whole other type of flames. As in, a poof of smoke and you left nothing but ashes behind. While the goggles protected me from any accidental basilisk glaring, they did nothing for my facial features. The strap of the unwieldy glasses went around my head and made my pointed ears stick out nearly parallel to the floor. I looked more like a devil than an elf. But I was required to wear them at all times inside the barn. Safety first and all that.

I leaned my shovel against the pen where I'd been cleaning out the basilisk stalls. Scholarship students had to earn their keep. And if I wanted to graduate with the credentials to go on and study mythological biology at university, I had to pay my dues and scoop the poop.

But why did I have to do it in front of Tatianna?

"Owen?" Her voice sent shivers down my spine and mortification rushing to my face. I was the only one on duty at the stables this afternoon. I sighed. There was no hiding.

"Owen, are you back there?" she called again.

"Coming!"

I squared my shoulders and took a breath and ignored the acrid smell of the scat on my boots.

"Hi, Tatianna, Savannah, Sloane." I nodded politely, squirming inside as the goggles weighted down my face and made my nod some bobbling jiggle. "What can I do for you ladies?"

Savannah tittered. "Owen, your eyeballs are bigger than a cyclops' in those goggles."

Because I wasn't self-conscious enough already.

Tatianna elbowed her friend and glared. A lash of flames flicked in her irises.

"Ignore her, Owen," Tatianna said. I nodded again, unsure. "I heard the baby basilisks were starting to hatch. I was hoping to take a look at them." She smiled, her face hopeful.

She was speaking to me. My tongue froze.

"I'm writing a paper on the life cycle of the basilisk, when they develop their venomous glare and stuff. Is it okay if we go back to the nesting area? I promise we'll stay far away. I just want to observe a while." She smiled winningly.

"I," I cleared my throat. "That should be fine."

Awesomely brilliant thing to say.

"Come on, I'll take you back." I reached under the counter by the entrance and pulled out several pairs of goggles.

"Ugh. Really?" Savannah grumbled. "The babies aren't even dangerous."

"Rules are rules," Sloane chimed in. "You could get an expulsion if a professor caught you in here without them on. Besides, who knows when the mother might make an appearance?" Sloane was ever a rule follower.

The girls followed me down the hay strewn aisle to the back corner where the nest of eggs was kept. There'd been a few hatchlings today and they weren't much bigger than large earth worms.

"Wow. Why did you choose to do your report on these ugly little wiggly things?" Savannah asked as Tatianna crouched to get a better look.

"They're interesting! How many other creatures can destroy you with one look?" Tatianna said.

"Uh, anything spawned by Medusa?" Savannah retorted.

Tatianna rolled her eyes, her flames waving behind the lenses. "Owen, do you know how many hatched this morning?"

I swallowed as her red-brown eyes tracked to mine behind the hideous goggles. Even with the eyewear, she was stunning. The goggles magnified her eyes, their natural glimmer enhanced. It made my knees weak.

"I think three this morning. A few more this afternoon," I stammered.

She nodded and we fell silent as we watched the baby basilisks.

Savannah grabbed the shovel I'd been using earlier and used the wooden end to prod a clump of hay out by itself in the nest area. "Is that a pile of...?"

"Stop!" I shouted.

Suddenly a loud hiss broke through the quiet of the barn and the hairs on the back of my neck stood on end.

"What is..." Savannah broke off with a scream as the mother basilisk launched herself straight for Savannah's face.

She flailed, her arm catching me just under the goggles.

"No!" I gasped as the momentum of her arm took the edge of the goggles off. I could smell the venom emanating from the crea-ture. Scales appeared in  front of my naked eyes as the creature catapulted towards me.

Sloane screamed.

"Oh, no you don't!" Tatianna's voice sounded far off.

She whipped off her goggles and a stream of white-hot flame jumped from her eyes and startled the mother basilisk.

It was the hottest thing I'd ever seen in my life. Literally and figuratively.

The basilisk slithered off, hissing and spitting.

Without words we legged it back to the barn entrance, quickly leaving the goggles on the desk and moving into the open air of the meadow beside the barn.

"Are you all right, Owen?" Tatianna asked, her flickering eyes full of concern that sent heat straight to my toes and had nothing to do with the inferno hiding inside her.

"I am, thanks to you," I admitted. I attempted a smile that she returned.

"Everyone else okay?" I asked. Sloane and Savannah nodded shakily.

"You girls go on back. I'll catch up," Tatianna nodded to her friends. Savannah still looked significantly shaken while Sloane looked smug as she glanced at us. She took Savannah's arm and led her back toward the dormitories.

"That was an impressive display of flames back there," I said, swallowing hard. "Thank you. You probably saved my life." The gravity of the situation was not lost on me.

Tatianna shrugged and tucked the corner of her bottom lip between her teeth.

"I feel kind of guilty. You wouldn't have been in that position at all if I hadn't asked to see the baby basilisks."

"It's fine. They're not off limits. Besides, didn't you want to research them?"

"Well, yes." She hesitated and glanced sideways at me. "But that's not the real reason I wanted to come see them."

"It's not?" My eyebrows hitched up my forehead. She looked up at me shyly under her long lashes.

"I actually just wanted to come hang out with you. The basilisks were an excuse."

My mouth fell open like a drop-jaw ready to consume its prey.

"Say something, Owen."

"You don't need the basilisks as an excuse."

"Yeah?" Her whole face brightened, and my heart thundered.

"Yeah," I whispered back with a smile so wide my cheeks hurt.

Tentatively I reached out and brushed her fingers. Hers tightened around mine and her eyes lit with an entirely different kind of fire as her mouth tipped up.

"Although maybe I could wash off the basilisk poop before we hang out?"

She giggled and set my heart on fire.

Magik Prep Academy

A
Spark
&
a
Wave

AJ Skelly

A SPARK & A WAVE

Oh, that was a powerful stench!

I fought the urge to wretch as the doors closed behind me, shutting me in with the odors of the subterranean pool.

Never again would I trust that red-headed scoundrel. It was his fault I was here, gasping for breath, gagging at the edge of the Kelpie pen.

"Hold this," he'd said. "I'll be right back," he'd said.

Were I not so new at this school, were I not so desperate to fit in after being kicked out of the last three schools I'd attended, were I not so distracted, I would have realized that the thing he handed me wasn't a wet suit. It was a Selkie skin. And said Selkie had come storming down the hallway in all her nakedness shooting sparks from her eyeballs and curses from her mouth not one minute later.

Guess who was left holding the bag. Literally.

My first week at Magik Prep Academy, and I was already serving detention. My punishment was to clean this stinking Kelpie pen. While taking care not to touch the beasts. Because they'd happily drag me down and eat me for dinner if I got too close. Wonderful.

I snapped on the long rubber gloves to protect my skin from the ick in the water and any accidental Kelpie grazing.

"My, aren't you a tasty looking morsel," a watery voice said.

I brandished my long-handled skimmer.

"Unless you want to swim around in your own muck, leave off, and let me do my job," I growled.

I was in no mood for teasing. Or for snacking. On me.

"She's a feisty one," another voice joined the first.

"Mm. I think the feisty ones have a nice spicy flavor," a third voice whinnied.

Three squelchy horse heads bobbed in the water, transparent, but fully corporeal. They weren't quite opaque, and I could see the tiled floor below them at the bottom of the pen. I poked at them with the bristled end along the outside edge of the skimmer.

The first one snapped its teeth at the bristles then reached out and clamped its watery teeth on the handle, nearly jerking me into the water with them. I let go and stumbled back, glaring at them.

"Fine. But I'm the only one scheduled to clean in here this week. Your choice. Algae or fresh water."

"Leave the poor girl alone," a new voice said.

I looked up in surprise at the deep male voice. A regal, watery horse head rose from the water, taller and larger than the others.

The three made loud whinnying noises that bordered on shrieking.

The male lunged up, spraying water everywhere as his front hooves churned the pool into frothy waves. The noise that echoed from his mouth sent the hairs on the back of my neck racing to attention and sent the other three Kelpies splashing into the dark water at the far side of the pool.

I sat, cowed and damp, against the wall, as far away from the beast as I could. The big Kelpie sunk back into the water up to his chest.

"Sorry about them. Brood mares." He seemed to roll his liquid eyes. I didn't move. I was thoroughly freaked out.

He gently swished to the abandoned skimmer. He clipped it with his teeth, and with a powerful fling of his head, tossed it back to land beside me.

"I certainly won't stand in your way." With a bob of his majestic head, he turned to submerge.

"Wait!"

His ears pricked forward as he turned back to me.

"Thank you."

The Kelpie inclined his head.

"You're welcome." He swam closer to the edge. "I'm Kai."

I swallowed, unsure if he was being nice to lure me to dinner, or because he wasn't as nasty as his female counterparts.

"Lara." I slowly got to my feet and retrieved the scrubber.

"Lara. I've not seen you here before. Toss me that short brush and I'll help. You can talk. We don't get many visitors in here."

I threw him the brush and set to work with my own pole, still wary and keeping the big Kelpie always within my sight.

"Tell me how your classes are going," Kai encouraged.

"Well, I only started three days ago."

"And you've already landed yourself with Kelpie clean up?" He snorted. I glared.

"It wasn't exactly my fault," I protested, feeling an unnatural urge to defend myself to this water creature.

"I'm all ears," he said as he scrubbed the tiles at the waterline. His ears twitched, dripping water, as if to accentuate his comment.

"Well, I have this...unique ability. Sometimes it does what it wants without my permission," I began. Without really meaning to say anything, the story came tumbling out. I was lonely. Lonelier than I'd realized. Kai didn't judge. He only listened.

"And that's why I was kicked out of the last school. I can't control it. It just bursts out whenever it feels like it. These giant fireballs. At my last school I accidentally lit the library on fire. That was the last straw. The headmaster said I had to go. So, here I am. At yet another school, hoping they can teach me how to control this energy inside me."

Kai looked at me. "I know it doesn't smell as nice to humanoids like you in here as it does to us, but there's nothing in here that you can burn up. If you suddenly start to spark, it's no trouble for me to send a little wave and put it out. You're welcome anytime."

I glanced up at him. This giant Kelpie somehow recognized the pain and loneliness echoing in my chest and homed in on it.

"You're not just inviting me...to be dinner?"

Kai snorted and slapped the surface of the pool with his soggy hoof. "If it makes you feel any better, I'm a vegetarian. The three harridans you met earlier would be happy to serve you on a seaweed sandwich, but not me. I'll make certain you're safe while you're here."

A spark flared to life in my chest and cinders formed at my fingertips and halos of flame began to materialize on my palms.

"Oh, no!"

A gentle mist appeared over my fingers, quieting the burn, and sending the scorching fire back to sleep inside me.

"See?"

Kai's eyes, though still see-through, held kindness. Something I had not expected from a Kelpie, given their questionable reputation.

"Why would you do this for me?"

"You are not the only one lonely on this campus, Lara."

I smiled. Maybe Magik Prep would be a good fit after all.

Magik Prep Academy

The Kraken Job

AJ Skelly

THE KRAKEN JOB

I hated Kraken class.

But my mom made me take it anyway. We came from a long line of Kraken Hunters, she said. I had to learn what I was meant to do, she said.

The trouble was, I didn't want to be in the family business. I didn't want to grow up and become a Kraken Slayer.

Honestly, I was kind of taken with the little beasties.

I sighed down at the tiny pool at my feet. Magik Prep Academy had one of the best Kraken cours- es available. We learned everything there was to know about them. I swished my finger in the pool and a baby tentacle wrapped around my finger.

I pried it loose with a gentle tug.

I thought maybe they could be useful. They had hidden talents. Possibly. Maybe they weren't just mindless killing machines once they reached adulthood.

I sighed again as I went to the simulation studio. It was my turn in the sim today. Everyone in the class had to take turns in the simulations. It was a major part of our training. Today I was bait and Kyle "Kraken Killer" (because everyone needs an alliterated nick name) was the slayer. We nodded to each other.

It didn't matter that it was all a simulation. My heart pounded every time I went into a one. The locations and entrapment situations changed with each sim. The magic flickered bright green, and I found myself wedged underneath the fallen beams of a ship. My legs were stuck. I couldn't even wiggle my toes.

"And START!" someone shouted. Magic shimmered again and I was suddenly surrounded by seawater, smoke, and there was a rubbery tentacle flying towards me. I bit back a scream and ducked my head under the fallen mast as the Kraken tentacle missed me by inches, shattering the deck and sending splinters shooting into my hair and embedding a few in my arm.

Gritting my teeth, I looked through the haze, my heart in my throat. Where was Kyle? The wood groaned beneath me and water flooded over my feet. Panic seized me and I desperately tried to kick my feet loose. Even though it was all a magic-induced sim, I would still feel the pain of drowning, or being eaten, or any other number of horrible Kraken-related disasters the sims produced.

The water rode up over my hips.

"Kyle!" I hollered.

A yelp pierced through the smoke and the Kraken shrieked.

Heavily suctioned and swinging with vengeance, a tentacle wrapped around my waist and hauled me skyward, far above the ship.

I cried out as my legs were wrenched from underneath the heavy beams and grunted as one boot came off and nearly took a toe with it.

"Hang on, Eiryn! I'm coming!" Kyle's call was far below and lost in the frothing sea and columns of smoke.

The Kraken screeched and the rubbery mass around my waist tightened painfully. Barely able to reach my foot, I gripped the little dagger still sheathed in my remaining boot. Yanking it out, I plunged the tiny weapon into the flesh surrounding my middle as it began cutting off my air supply. The blade didn't do much damage, but the creature loosened its hold enough that I could draw a full breath.

"Kyle!" I shouted again.

"Almost there!"

I hated being the bait.

But I hated killing the sim Krakens, too. I wondered if the beasts were inherently evil because

all we ever saw them do was take down ships and eat sailors—or did they do that because we blundered into their territory and sailors were tasty?

A scream tore from my lips as the tentacle suddenly released me and I went plummeting.

"Kill it before I hit the water, will you?" I screamed as I plunged through the air. The water raced to meet me, and it was going to hurt like nobody's business if I smacked into the surface. It might even kill me in the sim, which would mean Kyle would lose his points, too. It would be bad for both of us.

The water was inches from my face, and I covered my head with my arms.

Just as I should have been obliterated on the surface of the sea, I fell heavily onto the rubber mats covering the sim room floor.

My chest was heaving and the stench of burning ash still clung to me.

Kyle was bent over, his hands braced on his knees, breathing hard.

"Sorry, Eiryn. I was right in its beak when the sim opened." He swiped a hand through his black hair.

"It's alright." My voice was weary.

He glanced at me, his eyes blue like deep water.

"You hate the sims, don't you?" he whispered.

It wasn't a secret that I didn't like them, but it wasn't something I broadcast around. Didn't want the family name to be sullied with my dislike.

I nodded.

He looked at me, really looked at me.

"Have lunch with me today. I want to talk to you."

"All right," I agreed, curiosity piqued.

I slid my tray next to Kyle's in the refectory and swished some purple threads of magic off my chair before sitting.

"So. What did you want to talk to me about?" I asked him as I cracked the seal on my everflower juice.

He finished his bite of kelp salad sandwich and pierced me with a look.

"I want to recruit you."

My eyebrows shot up my forehead. "Recruit me for what?"

He paused a minute, scrutinizing me. "It's an experimental thing. There are several of us here on campus, and a few professors, who have been doing more research into the Kraken as a species. We want to set up a breeding program and breed Krakens that exhibit certain traits."

"To what end?"

"To see if we can't train them to help in rescue missions—retrieve sailors and ships that are in trouble instead of causing the catastrophes. Train them to retrieve artifacts, to go places we can't with our limitations."

I was hooked. Kyle was literally speaking everything I'd been thinking over the course of the past year.

"Why do you want me?" I sat intrigued, my lunch momentarily forgotten.

"I've seen the way you look in sims when you're the slayer, the way you handle the baby ones. I think you're sympathetic, even though your grandfather was the most famous slayer ever to graduate the Academy."

I smiled. "Count me in."

Magik Prep Academy
A
Bit of
Magic
&
Advice
AJ Skelly

A Bit of Magik & Advice

"No one cares for the Brownies anymore. Not a care for us wee folk," I grumbled as I swept my broom over the dusty hall. The stones of Magik Prep Academy had soaked up magic for centuries. Unfortunately, that did diddly poot to dislodge the dirt and grime from all those students traversing the corridors during the day.

I grunted as my lower back twinged again. I straightened and narrowly missed slinging my long white beard right into the bucket of soapy water.

"What next," I muttered. "Soon they'll forget to feed me and then I'll have every reason to scratch this cleaning agreement." I yanked my beard out of the way and stomped, then coughed as a cloud of powdery violet magic came loose.

Rolling my eyes, I swirled my finger in the air and made the magic useful. The loose bits flung themselves down and scattered the dirt into the air.

Cupping my hands like a funnel, I forced the air through and brought the dust whirling in like a tornado straight into my waiting bucket.

Nodding in satisfaction I shook my beard out where a stray string of green magic clung like a barnacle.

"Off, you pesky thing!" I frowned at the offending string and would have said more to it, but my overly large ears picked up the faintest sniffle.

Odd. It was far too late for students to still be afoot. They should all be tucked away at the dormitories or off doing whatever mischief teenage creatures did. Only we Brownies and the old ogre that made up the cleaning staff were still in the Academy proper at this time of night.

Finding the sniffle of more interest than polishing the flagstones, I hobbled off in the direction of the interruption.

I passed half a dozen empty classrooms and finally came to the cloistered courtyard—open to the air and wreathed in the magenta glow from the fading sunlight. And there, huddled miserably against an ancient stone wall, was a lump.

A large lump compared to me.

"I say, why you be here?" I called up to the lump when I was within speaking distance.

A head jerked up, tear tracks visible on the pale cheeks.

"Books and bluster, you're a faun. What you be doing here? It's after hours, laddie." I tapped my foot for emphasis.

The young faun just looked at me, surprise and maybe a dash of fear lingering in the dark brown eyes below the mop of curly hair and little horn buds.

"I...what *are* you?" His whispered words quivered.

"Bless my buttons and saints preserve us! What do they teach at this school? I'm a *Brownie*. Have ye never heard of us wee folk?"

"Oh. I'm sorry. I'm new here." He cleared his throat. "No, I've never seen a Brownie."

I lifted a bushy eyebrow.

"But I read about one once?" he offered hopefully. "Am I in trouble?"

I rolled my eyes and blew a raspberry through my lips.

"And what be a young laddie like yerself be doing out here at this time o' the evening?" I didn't like repeating myself, but the poor thing looked right miserable.

He scrubbed his wet cheeks then wrapped his arms around his knees.

"It's my first time here—at boarding school. I...I was feeling a little homesick. I didn't want the other boys to see."

"Aye. The sun always shines brighter on the morrow. There, there. Haven't ye got any friends here?"

The brown curls shook, and his lips tugged down.

"No. I'm the eldest of my clan. I'm the first since my parent's generation to board here at Magik Prep. And it's not that I'm ungrateful!" he added quickly. Attending the Academy was a great honor, good he recognized it. "I'm just...lonely. I've never been away from home. The other fauns have been here longer. They all know each other and know all the rules of the school. I don't."

Poor lad was lonesome. I knew how that was. My old cantankerous heart stretched a mite as a seed of compassion bloomed.

"I know how that is, laddie. Ye didn't know me now, did ye? Most folks have forgotten us Brownies even exist. And for the most part, so long as we're fed, we're happy to go on about our business. But it does get lonely, being forgotten."

The faun nodded.

"I tell you what. You see this stubborn string of green magic here?" I tugged the silly thing free of my beard and coiled it around my finger. "You take this here to class with you tomorrow. You put it in your hand and see if it doesn't point to another lonesome student. Then the two of you can befriend each other. There's no rules saying you have to keep to yer own kind. Magik Prep has more mix breeds and off shoots and oddities than I've got whiskers." I shook my heavy white beard with a knowing nod, then placed the coil of magic into his hand. His eyes lit up like I'd given him a great treasure. I sprinkled a dash of my own Brownie magic on the coil to be sure it behaved itself.

"Thank you," he said reverently.

I patted his hoof. "You go find yourself a friend. And if no one else in the whole school is lonely, you just come on back here and I'll keep you company meself." I cracked a rare grin.

"I will. Even if I find a friend. I mean, if you'd like the company."

A laugh bubbled right up. "What be your name, boy?"

"Alek."

"Pleased to meet ye, Alek. You go on. You may see me from time to time. I'll be around if you need."

"Thank you, Mr..."

"Milis. Just plain old Milis."

"I will remember you, Mr. Milis." The brown eyes held a sincerity that I hadn't seen in a long time and it warmed my old bones right down to the marrow.

"You go on now, before it gets full dark, young Alek. Go find someone tomorrow that needs a friend worse than ye."

A smile tipped one corner of his mouth.

I found an odd jaunt in my steps the next evening as I cleaned. I hurried with my regular chores, intent on checking for my lump of a friend.

He was not there, but what he left behind brought a smile to my lips and set my belly grumbling.

I picked up the note, which was nearly as large as me.

Mr. Milis,

I haven't forgotten you. I used your green magic coil today and I think I've made a friend. I was invited to go dragon watching tonight, but I didn't want you to be lonely either. I did some research, and Brownies are supposed to love cream. I hope this is all right.

I'll visit you soon.

Thank you.

-Alek

Mr. Milis,

I haven't forgotten you. I used your green magic coil today and I think I've made a friend. I was invited to go dragon watching tonight, but I didn't want you to be lonely either. I did some research, and Brownies are supposed to love cream. I hope this is all right.

I'll visit you soon.

Thank you.

-Alek

I inhaled the sweet aroma from the bowl of fresh cream and smiled to myself.

Not forgotten, indeed.

Magik Prep Academy
A Screech & a Click
AJ Skelly

A Screech & a Click

Time is running out.

So help me, if I can't get this stupid locker open and retrieve my dragon's muzzle, I can't go to my Dragon Hatcher's Apprenticeship class. And if I miss one more class, I'll be kicked out of the program, and my life-long dream of becoming a full-fledged dragon hatcher will go up in smoke.

I resist the urge to glare at Simone, my hatchling dragon, as she perches innocently on my shoulder. Her humming sends vibrations down my arm. I was so proud of her sweet little purple-scaled body the first day I brought her into class. Then she opened her mouth.

And the most hellish sound ever heard in the history of the Tri Kingdoms blasted from her skinny little body.

Professor Injar's hands clamped around his pointed ears so fast my eyes couldn't even track the movement. Of course, I was just as shocked as everyone else. Simone had been a model hatchling up to that point, making only quiet little mewling noises no louder than a cat's purr. But not in Apprenticeship class. Oh, no.

I still haven't figured out what it is about the room that sets her off, but every time we enter, she squawks her fool head off.

Professor Injar has since forbidden her entrance into the class unless she wears her muzzle. And since I'm not permitted to class without my dragon, I have to get this stupid locker open.

I kick the bottom of the impenetrable metal cabinet—I'm that frustrated. I yank on the lock again, to no avail.

With all the threads of magic weaving down this hallway, you'd think one of them would be helpful. The old stone walls of Magik Prep Academy leach the charmed substance into the air, but it's forbidden to use for what the administration calls *nefarious purposes*. Otherwise, I'd whip that piece of yellow magic floating to my right over here, bend it a few times, and shove it into the bottom of the lock. Boom. Spring the lock, get the muzzle, pass my apprenticeship class.

But no. If I were to do that and a teacher caught me, I'd be kicked out of the Academy long enough my grades would plummet. I'm about to risk it anyway, because I'm going to fail the class one way or the other at this point.

Simone rubs her little horned head affection-ately against my cheek.

"You know this is all your fault," I mutter as I spin the dial once more, trying desperately to hear the clicks that will tell me the tumblers have moved inside.

It's no use. There's just too much noise in the hallway, and my lock is too finnicky.

I should have sprung the extra ten darrits and bought a bio lock, but I'd used the cash I saved to buy the upgraded muzzle instead. The one with the enhanced silencer.

Oh, the irony.

"All right, come on, come on," I mutter under my breath. My fingers give the dial the barest brush of movement.

"Yes!" One tumbler moved. I heard it with my left ear strained against the cool metal of my locker.

Simone belches a thin trickle of smoke next to my right ear.

"Not helping, Simone."

Green light zings down the threads of magic in the hallway, and my heartbeats kick up another notch. It's the five-increment warning light. I have to get this lock off. *Now*.

I press my ear as close to the lock as I can and bite back a curse as another student laughs loudly behind me. I mash my cheek into the locker, knocking my glasses  askew. Someone trips over my backpack at my feet and thumps into me.

"Sorry, Bryon. You okay?"

It's Lyra Songstrum. One of the most gorgeous girls at the Academy. I spend half of Apprenticeship class trying not to stare at her. Could this day get any more humiliating?

"Here. Your glasses are all crooked." She reaches out and straightens them.

My face flames, my heart pounds, and I wish I could melt into the floor. "Fine," I mumble, even more flustered now that Lyra is watching me try to get my stupid lock undone.

"It's stuck?"

Obviously.

I clear my throat. "Yeah," I mutter lamely.

Miraculously, I feel more than hear the next tumbler click into place. Sweat breaks out on my forehead as purple light streaks down the hall. Two increments! Only one more tumbler left.

I move the dial, Lyra peering over my shoulder. I move it, but it doesn't click. I just can't hear it! A frustrated growl builds in my chest. "It's so *loud* in here!"

"Oh. I can help with that," Lyra says. With that, she plucks Simone from my shoulder, points her in the general direction of the hallway, and gives her purple tail a quick pinch.

Simone screams her devil cry. As I wince, a shocked hush falls over the hall.

I waste no time. With delicate fingers, I move the dial just a hair to the left.

Click.

Relief floods me as I yank the door open and Simone's upgraded silencer muzzle tumbles out. I swear, I'm getting a bio lock tonight.

"All good?" Lyra smiles as noise slowly swells again in the corridor.

"All good," I echo, shoving my glasses back up my nose and looping the muzzle over Simone's tiny mouth.

My future career as a dragon hatcher has been saved.

Magik Prep Academy

Blundering with Basilisks

AJ Skelly

BLUNDERING WITH BASILISKS

Colin "Hunter" Abreen was my brother's best friend, the best basilisk hunter instructor at Magik Prep Academy, and definitely off limits. My treacherous heart needed more persuasion on that last part; I'd been in love with him since I was twelve. Once or twice, I'd even thought I'd seen him looking at me like I looked at him. It was enough to give me hope.

On a stupid whim I'd signed myself up for Colin's 401 Basilisk Hunter course as my senior elective. Apparently, I was a glutton for punishment. And a hopeless basilisk hunter. I'd been sent to the infirmary with fang punctures more times than anyone else.

Ever.

In the entire history of the class.

It didn't matter how hard I tried, how often I practiced my technique, or how desperately I wanted to excel and impress Colin. I just couldn't see the stupid, villainous creatures. But they always saw me. And then they bit me.

My pointed ears twitched; my blonde hair was pulled up and out of the way so nothing would hinder my ability to hear their soft slithering. My elf ears were more reliable than my eyesight in picking out their inconspicuous bodies in the dense underbrush of the Academy's forested park. Even using my enhanced vision goggles that protected me from the dangerous stare of the loathsome beasts, my ears were a better bet.

My fingers gripped my net and my hooked stick. I would catch this basilisk if it was the last thing I did. We'd been stalking each other in circles for the past seventy-eight increments. I was done stalking. I was ready to conquer.

A slither to the right!

No, there, in the bush!

I silently raised my net and hook, ready to scoop up the smarmy, slithery, insufferable creature. Crouching as Colin had instructed, I crept forward with the grace of a sleek-bodied water nymph.

A slight movement!

Gotcha!

I howled and dropped my net that had snared a terribly dangerous patch of wildflowers and clutched my hand. My whole arm smarted as the creature's mild venom spread needle-like tingles up to my shoulder. Glancing at the bushy fronds in front of me, I just made out the basilisk's disappearing tail.

Biting back a curse, I glanced at my hand. It wasn't a bad bite. But it was a bite. And I'd failed yet again to capture a reptilian fiend.

I ripped off my goggles and stomped toward the instructor tent set up at the opening of the woods.

Colin looked up from his desk, and I swear a smile flitted across his face as I came crashing out of the underbrush. If only that smile meant he was glad to see me and not because I required a triple dose of patience and more repeated instruction than anyone else in the class.

"Again, Kaebre?"

My shoulders slumped in defeat. "Again."

"Let me see."

I held my hand out for his inspection. When he took it carefully in his large rough ones, I suppressed a shiver and hoped he didn't notice. He turned my palm over and then back to the marred skin by my knuckles. I watched his face as he examined my hand, but he kept his eyes on the bite mark.

"Come on. These are just scratches. I can patch these up myself with the first aid kit here."

He led me over to a stump where I sagged like a bag of bones. I felt like a child who wanted desperately to gain their teacher's approval. Except I wanted more than Colin's approval. I wanted him to look at me the way I had looked at him since he and my brother had let me tag along, climbing trees in the back yard together. A heavy sigh escaped my lungs.

"Cheer up, Kaebre. Basilisk hunting isn't for everyone. So long as you capture one before the term ends, you'll pass the course."

Mortification slid through me, and I clenched my teeth to keep my chin from quivering. I was humiliated. Pathetic. I was the only student in the course not to have netted a basilisk. Fresh worry for my grade slid over the humiliation.

"How did you become so good so quick-ly?" I asked him quietly. "You broke every basilisk-catching record within six weeks of starting the course, and now, the year after your own graduation, you're the instructor. Top universities around the country are trying to recruit you for their basilisk programs. Col, how did you do it?"

He was still a minute, his broad shoulders moving slowly as he took a breath. His shaggy thatch of bronze hair grazed over his forehead in the slight breeze. His head was bent, his fingers carefully tying off the gauze around my hand. He stilled even more; his body like chiseled marble bowed over my hand.

Slowly he tipped his head so that his blue eyes met mine. My breath caught, and my heart sped up as he locked gazes with me. His hands still engulfed mine.

"Kaebre," he started, then paused.

My eyebrows rose, encouraging him, and my fingers squeezed his lightly before I could stop them.

"I'm about to tell you something that is not common knowledge. I'd like to keep it that way."

I nodded. He was trusting me with sensitive information. Was it possible I'd worked my way up from best friend's little sister to reliable student — and maybe his friend in my own right?

He glanced around, ensuring we were alone before meeting my eyes again.

"I'm color blind. Completely."

I cocked my head, the full weight of his words slowly registering. Color blind? It was a rare genetic trait. Rare, undesired, and dangerous in a world filled with colored magic. Use the wrong color and you could kill yourself or somebody else.

But how did that help him catch basilisks?

The corner of his mouth tipped at my confusion.

"Their camouflage isn't camouflage to me. I see everything in black, white, and grey. Without their colors to blend in, it's easy to spot their markings between the leaves and the underbrush."

I was stunned as my thoughts caught up.

"You've hid it your whole life."

He nodded.

"I can't see colors, but I can see other things." He ran his thumb over my knuckles, carefully avoiding my wound, and my face flamed.

He chuckled.

"I'll make a deal with you. You catch a basilisk, pass the course, and when you graduate in a month, we'll talk about the becoming shade of grey on your face right now."

He squeezed my hands as my eyes sparkled. My smile stretched across my face, but I didn't care. Not anymore. I'd already waited years for Colin to notice me. Now that I knew he had, graduation wasn't so far away.

I just had to catch a basilisk. Hidden, wretched, heinous creatures.

"I will catch a basilisk if I have to do it with my teeth."

Colin laughed, a deep noise that rumbled up from his chest and set goose flesh loose over my skin.

"Look for the patterns on their skin. I can't replicate my condition for you, but I really, really want you to catch that basilisk and graduate."

He winked and my heart did summer saults.

I would be the best late-blooming basilisk hunter Magik Prep Academy had ever seen.

One more month.

Disclosure

AJ Skelly

DISCLOSURE

The Winter Gala.

The one Magik Prep Academy function I'd been dreaming of for weeks. Tonight was the night Tyler Crawson would notice me.

I'd had a crush on him for ages but lacked the courage to do anything about it. Not tonight. With bravery I didn't feel, I stepped boldly into the great hall.

Music pealed and lights twinkled. Bright strands of magic floated effortlessly through the air, only to be soaked up by the ancient stone walls now festooned with tinsel and evergreen. More multi-colored strings of magic hovered over the carved rock.

With my best friend Aida next to me and her earlier pep talk still ringing in my ears, I gulped, trying to calm my frantic heartbeat.

"You've got this, Girl." Aida winked at me. The flashing red and green lights bounced off her caramel-colored skin. Her ebony hair, curled tight as springs, absorbed the lights and shadows alike. I wished it would absorb my anxiety.

"Breathe, Lainey." She looked me over once more and nodded in satisfaction. "That blue sequin dress is perfect. You sparkle like fairy dust." Her plump lips pursed, and she reached behind me and plucked a thread of opalescent magic from the air and swished it around the hem of my dress. She snatched a golden thread near the bottom of the make-shift bleachers where we stood and wrapped it around my white-blonde hair, piled on top of my head. Tucking the end behind the long point of my ear, she smiled. "There. Now you're radiant."

A bronze head bobbed on the other side of the room. My heart seized.

Target acquired.

My knees knocked and sweat ghosted my palms.

"I'm going to go make sure the werewolves

haven't spiked the punch." Aida was on the social committee. The werewolves generally liked to party...alternatively to committee plans. With a final squeeze to my shoulder, she was off, and I was left staring at Tyler's head as it dipped and weaved throughout the crowd.

The music was loud. Too loud. It vibrated up my legs.

I swept up a handful of my shimmery skirt so my feet wouldn't tangle in the hem. The opalescent string of magic soaked into my dress, straightening my back, and giving me confidence while the golden strand had a calming effect on my poor ragged heart.

I'd only gone a few bodies deep into the crowd when a hand reached out and snatched mine.

"Kieran!" I gasped as my other best friend released me.

"Lainey. Wow. You look…" he trailed off as his eyebrows rose to his black hairline. He was all dark where I was light. I couldn't tell if it was the red lights or if the points of his ears colored slightly.

Searching the crowd again, I found Tyler's head. He was only a few yards to my right.

"Looking for Tyler?" Kieran broke in dryly.

"Yes. Tonight he's finally going to see me as more than the smart girl in math class." I practically hissed the words between my teeth.

Kieran's expression soured. "You don't want him, Lainey. You really don't."

Anger and the sting of unintended betrayal crept into my belly. I glared at Kieran. Wasn't he supposed to be on my side?

"Lainey Rowan? Wow, looking hot, babe!"

The voice froze my blood and Kieran could probably see the whites of my eyes.

Plastering a smile on my face that I hoped didn't look deranged, I turned.

"Hey, Tyler." My voice came out higher than it should have. Maybe he didn't notice over the boom of the music.

Without any preamble, Tyler grabbed my hand and put his other low on my waist and swung me onto the dance floor. Kieran grunted somewhere behind me.

We danced for long glorious moments. I was in ecstasy. The song wasn't particularly slow, but it wasn't fast. We moved together, faster than a slow dance, but no weird gyrating. Which was fine, because it let me savor every second of

Tyler's hands on my waist without worrying if I was writhing appropriately to the music.

When the song ended, Tyler's copper-colored eyes gazed into mine. My hand fisted into his lapel without my permission. A smile crooked his lips as his eyes roved over my face and one eyebrow rose.

Slowly he leaned down and let his lips caress my cheek. Figurative fireworks blasted out my ears.

"Don't go anywhere," he whispered huskily against my ear. "I'll be back in a few." His big hand squeezed my side before his fingers slowly trailed away.

I'm pretty sure I grew roots right there on the parquet floor.

I don't know how long I stood there like an idiot in the middle of the room, but I came to when Kieran tugged on my hand.

"Kieran, did you see?" I sighed. "He's glorious."

Kieran snorted, his dark elf side showing in his pessimism. His forehead furrowed, his heavy black brows hanging low over his eyes as his mouth tugged into a thin line.

"You need to see something," he muttered as he grabbed my hand and pulled me through the throng of students and out the arched doorway into the quiet corridor.

Kieran stopped us beside one of the heavy tapestries that lined the antechambers outside the great hall. A string of purple magic clung to the bottom of my sparkly skirt.

"Look. I..." he trailed off and ran a hand through his black hair. "I don't want to show you this but consider the truth my gift to you this year."

My eyebrows drew together again as he pulled me down the passageway. We crept to the end where it was deserted. His gaze met mine as he put a long finger against his lips, then motioned with his head for me to look around the corner.

Unsure, I peeked out just enough to get an eyeful.

My hand flew to my silent mouth.

There was the boy who'd kissed me moments before. Who had looked at me like I was the center of the world. The boy on whom I'd hung my hopes.

He was necking a gorgeous red-head. And his hands...were not appropriately placed. My eyes burned as I turned and fled soundlessly back down the ancient corridor, kicking up a dusting of magic in my wake.

I sagged onto a stone bench in a deserted hallway—far away from the snogging couple—who for all I knew were no longer snogging and had moved on to other things. I swiped angrily under one eye. Kieran slowly sat beside me.

"I'm sorry, Lainey. I know you liked him. He doesn't *see* you. Doesn't know how special you are." He hesitated and swallowed hard. "Maybe you should look at someone who has seen you all along."

The sincerity in his tone jerked my gaze to his. His chocolate brown eyes swam with vulnerability, and my heart lurched painfully in my chest.

Because he *did* see me.

Kieran had *always* seen me. He'd seen me when I was all awkward limbs and angles. When I won the science award. When I burned my bangs off with a spell gone wrong. When I dropped chocolate frosting all down my shirt. When my gran passed away. He'd seen *me*.

A heaviness around my heart lifted as I stared at his face, my eyes tracing every line of his messy hair, his pointed ears, his strong jaw, his dark eyes fringed in thick lashes, the tilt of his lips. The intensity and vulnerability in his eyes.

"I see you, Lainey," he whispered roughly.

And for the first time, I saw him, too.

Magik Prep Academy
Spiking
the
Punch
AJ Skelly

SPIKING THE PUNCH

"They better not have spiked the punch. So help me, I will end the whole pack of them!" I muttered under my breath as I swished to the refreshments table in my long satin dress. It was the big formal Christmas dance at Magik Prep Academy, and I was head of the refreshment committee for this event.

The werewolves made it their job to disrupt every social gathering, and I refused to let it happen on my watch.

My stomach lurched as I approached the table bordering the stage. There he was. Corbin

Fang. Tall, gorgeous, blue eyed, and cold heart-ed. He'd just moved here and already he was causing waves in the pack hierarchy.

I tucked a tightly wound piece of dark hair be-hind my ear, snagging a piece of floating magic and weaving it into my wild, unruly mane to keep it in place. Flames threatened to erupt from my eyes as my anxiety heightened. As surreptitious-ly as possible, I dipped a strand of orange magic into the punch and sighed in relief when it didn't change color. All was safe for the moment.

"Everything spit spot?" Corbin sauntered up and his accent made my belly flip. I frowned.

"Just making sure every student has the chance to drink without belching fire or singeing their date," I returned. I glared. His blue eyes danced. "Last year your werewolf buddies put fire powder in the punch. Do you know what that does to poor unsuspecting creatures?"

"I heard about that one." His eyes twinkled.

I glared at him.

"Dance with me Uptight Girl."

"Excuse me?"

"Dance with me."

As if I would ever.

"I can't. I have to make sure the punch stays legal."

He snorted. "I'll take care of that. Hiya!" he called to several other werewolves lounging against the stage looking shifty. "Not a drop in the bowl. Understood?"

One of them bared his teeth and another snarled, but at a hard look from Corbin, heads bobbed. I refused to admit I was impressed.

He was the newly appointed junior alpha of the school-aged werewolves, according to the gossip. Looked like maybe the rumors were true.

Corbin grabbed my hand and tugged. I didn't budge. My eyes grew rounder.

"Come on. It'll be fun. You can lambast the finer points of being a werewolf while we dance." His eyes held a hidden mirth while his comment stung. I felt fire rising in my eyes and blinked it away. Not fast enough.

"Hey now. You've got gorgeous eyes. Flames in your veins?"

I sighed. "Phoenix. Pure. Both sides of the family." Why was I rambling such nonsense? It definitely wasn't because this furry cur had any effect on me. None whatsoever.

"That's fantastic! Tell me about it. Whilst we dance."

It was the accent. It did me in. I let him tug me away from the table to the dance floor. I cast one more look at the bowl of punch and the werewolves pacing not far away.

"If they put something in there and another fairy grows a tail this year, I will,"

He cut me off. "Relax. I told them not to. They're honor bound to obey me." His hand slid around my waist, and I barely contained a shiver.

"Really?" Did my voice waver?

"Really. Pack law. I may be the new guy, but I'm also the alpha guy. In our bloodlines, Fire Girl."

"Aida."

"Aye?"

"No. Aida. My name."

"I know." He winked and I bristled. "I've known your name since the second day I got here."

I wasn't sure if I should be flattered or consider him a stalker. I looked at him, trying to hide my general disgust. Werewolves were all trouble-makers. The whole lot of them. Corbin Fang was their leader.

"You know, we're not all that bad. Some of us are, sure, but not all," he said, seeming to read my mind.

I digested his words as he spun me around the floor, graceful but firm. Was I the one who was being narrow-minded?

"Which kind are you?" I finally asked as he twirled me once more.

"I'd tell you, but I don't think you'll believe me unless you figure it out for yourself." Was that a challenge in his eyes?

"Just like you are more than the fire inside you, there's more to me than fur and claws."

I bit my lip. I felt my own phoenix blood stirring. I hated it when people made assumptions about me because my eyes sometimes glowed. But preconceived notions were often helpful in dealing with the mythical community. At least, that's what I told myself as Corbin led me off the dance floor. His easy grip projected an inner confidence I envied.

We made it back to the punch table. I quickly dipped a strand of orange magic in and sighed in relief when it remained unchanged.

Corbin tisked playfully beside me as he filled two goblets. He snatched a strand of light blue magic from the air, split it, twisted it, and swirled it into the two cups. The punch glowed. It was beautiful.

"Here you go, Aida, my uptight fire girl who secretly wants to let her inner bird fly."

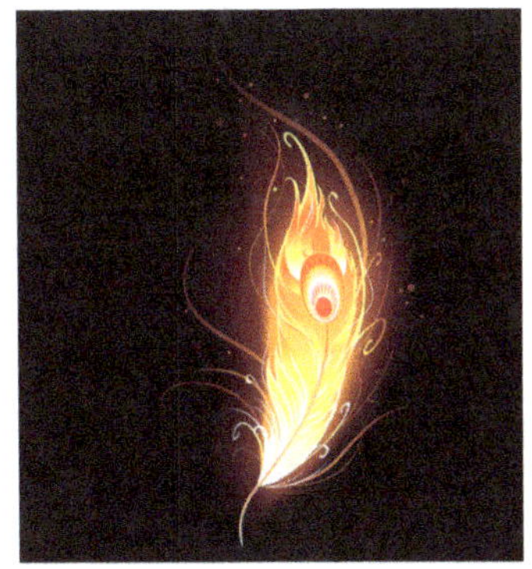

I gulped. How did he see me so well?

"What happens if I drink this?"

"It'll make your phoenix fire glow and give you a secondary sight for a while. You might see that some people are different than the sum of the rumors surrounding them."

He winked at me and tipped back his glass. His deep eyes stared back at me and slowly turned electric blue.

"You're just as beautiful on the inside as you are the outside. Although your insides are still tangled up in knots." He quirked a smile at me as he finished his assessment. Blood rushed to my cheeks. "What'll it be, Aida? Do you want to see me?"

The sudden desire to know who this boy was had me abandoning my cautious nature and tipping my glass back as well.

My fire woke within me. It rushed through me like sparklers in my blood. I buzzed with magic and knew the instant it hit my eyes. I sucked in a breath and looked at Corbin.

I gasped. He radiated goodness. Not the snark, not the alpha, not the rotten werewolf I imagined. His heart was kind, his intentions honorable.

I saw *him*.

"Merry Christmas, Aida."

"Merry Christmas, Corbin."

The Unicorn, Yggdrasil, & the Kiss

Magik Prep Academy

AJ Skelly

THE UNICORN, YGGDRASIL, & THE KISS

FENNRICK

Who did after school projects on a Friday? I kicked the toe of my boot against the dirt path, bemoaning Etta's absence. Some Academy friends and a gaggle of female werewolves hiked beside me. Including Etta's cousin, Lexie, who couldn't keep her hands to herself.

It wasn't entirely her fault. At eighteen and next in line to be Alpha, my body was beginning to secrete its own kind of Alpha pheromones. They tended to drive the unpaired females into a sort of frenzy anytime they were around me.

It was exhausting being the only eligible wolf man.

Cariss smiled apologetically. She'd been the one to invite me after school with promises that Etta would likely be coming. But her sister's honey-blonde ponytail was missing.

"Fennrick," Lexie cooed. "Tell me more about becoming an Alpha." Her fingers fluttered near my arm. I resisted the urge to roll my eyes.

"Well, I'm taking a few classes for it this semester. Brushing up on diplomacy, leadership, that sort of stuff." I rubbed the back of my neck. I was trying to practice some of those diplomatic skills on Lexie. She didn't even go to Magik Prep Academy. Although she was thinking about transferring next semester. I really hoped my budding Alpha genes weren't the cause.

"But what's it actually like?"

Grueling, I thought. "Dad and I spend a lot of time together, which is nice. He's teaching me everything not covered in the books."

She smiled and batted her eyelashes.

"Fenn, did you catch the game last night?" Owen, an elf friend, attempted to save me.

"I did," I replied. Probably with more enthusiasm than I needed as I broke away from Lexie to walk beside him.

We hiked another half hour before the pulsating threads of magic surrounding Yggdrasil—the tree where all the magic in our world originated—thrummed in my chest. Yggdrasil was a popular destination. Touching the tree was forbidden but basking in its glow was encouraged.

We rounded the final bend and there Yggdrasil sat in all its glory. *Stunning.* I propped a foot against the low guard railing and took it in. An array of magnificent colors flew from its branches, tangling, weaving into the sky to form a multi-colored halo of magic around the tree.

Every time I visited, the awe was fresh. I closed my eyes and breathed deeply, the scent of pure magic washing over me and filling that aching tiredness inside.

"It's beautiful, isn't it?" Lexie said as she joined me at the railing. She'd stayed next to me the whole hike, peppering me with questions, scenting me frequently, though I don't think she knew I could tell.

I nodded.

"Fennrick, did you know my grandpa was an Alpha, too?"

I stared at her, confused where this conversation was going. She stepped closer, her arm brushing mine and sending the hairs on the back of my neck standing on end.

"Lexie," I started.

"Kiss me, Fenn. Seal our fate together here, beneath the most magical place in our world."

Shock dropped my mouth open as my eyes bulged in their sockets. She must have taken it as encouragement because she leaned in.

My brain froze. I did not want Lexie's lips on mine. She knew werewolf tradition dictated that I save any kisses for the one who would be the recipient of *all* my kisses, but my body was sluggish, refusing to move.

"Lexie!" Cariss grabbed Lexie's arm. "*What* are you doing?"

Lexie shot Cariss a murderous glare and yanked her arm away. But as she did, the back of her legs hit the low guard rail.

In stupefied horror, I reached to grab her before she fell, but I wasn't fast enough.

Lexie toppled right over the edge of the railing and hit the curling roots of Yggdrasil. Her scream pierced the air as her back smacked onto the roots and an amber glow immediately encased her.

Lightening cracked across the sky as a violent wind whipped through Yggdrasil's leaves, sending a rush of them over us. The colored threads of magic flickered and lost their curving waves, becoming jagged, harsh, and static.

Thunder boomed.

"Lexie!" Cariss shrieked.

The sky opened. Rain, hail, and flickering bits of magic sizzled onto the ground.

"We've got to get out of here!" someone shouted.

"What about Lexie?" Owen called over the din.

"We have to leave her," Cariss said. Terror clouded her face as her eyes met mine.

There was nothing we could do for her. We couldn't pull her back. The magical amber glow encased her completely. I glanced at Lexie's face.

Her eyes were rounded in shock, her mouth an unmoving gash of horror. Her hands were stiff, fingers splayed as if to catch her fall. Amber light pulsated over her prone form.

A leaf whacked into my cheek, breaking into my racing thoughts.

"Cariss is right. We have to go get help." The Alpha part of me took charge. "Go. Back down the path. Now." A forceful growl punctuated my words.

We'd just unleashed fury like our world had never seen.

We raced ahead of the storm, trying desperately to beat the roiling waves of magic and angry lightening back to the Academy—to warn the others, and find Headmaster Capra. If anyone would know what to do, it would be him.

"Move it, Owen!" Cariss shouted as gravel spun beneath the tires of his Jeep. The other cars followed as we sped far faster than was healthy down the backroads.

"No signal. Anyone else have a signal?" I asked as I jammed my finger over the home screen on my cell phone.

"Nothing," Cariss replied, a slight edge of hysteria in her voice.

Breaking all speed regulations, we were back at school within fifteen minutes. The magic that normally lazed dormant in the hallways like little strings of colored light, frizzed and sparked. Centuries-old magic rose from the stones like a thick cloud of dust.

Leaping from the car before it came to a complete stop, I flinched as screams echoed from inside. A young centaur burst through the double doors and galloped out of the parking lot.

"Go check in with the pack; tell Dad what happened," I ordered the rest of the girls as they pulled in. Without question they peeled back out of the parking lot.

"Etta!" Cariss shrieked as a honey-blonde head appeared.

My heart slammed in my chest. She was still here. Tatianna, Owen's girlfriend, came rushing out behind her.

"Cariss! Something's happened! The magic! It's unstable! Everything is changing!" Etta yelled as we covered the distance between the front doors and the vehicles. Etta's wide blue-green eyes were large in her face, her freckles standing out sharply against her pale skin. Her gaze flitted to me. My hands twitched to reassure her, though all I could offer were empty words.

"I know. I think it might be partly my fault," Cariss hiccupped. "Lexie's encased in Yggdrasil."

"*What*?" Etta said, dumbfounded.

"Come on." I ushered them back towards the building, surprised how the urge to take charge just came out.

"Tatianna, have you seen Professor Capra?" Owen asked, grabbing her hand. We jogged and were quickly back in the building where several students ran through the halls. Magic careened and dipped, smashing wildly into the stone walls, sending showers of spangles dashing into the air.

"Let's try his office." Tatianna's eyes sparked with her inner phoenix fire. She was on the edge of her control. We all were. Fur prickled under my skin.

Sprinting through the ancient halls, we dodged shards of magic. Busting around a corner, disturbing phantom-like shadows wailed and scraped their ghoulish fingers towards us.

"What are those?" Etta gasped as I pulled her back around the corner, out of their reach.

"I don't know, but I don't think they're a natural phenomenon." My hand fell to the small of her back, herding her to the center and taking the outside edge of the group.

"They've got to be a product of this insanity." Cariss batted a torpedo of neon magic out of the way.

Owen jerked the door to the main office open.

"Duck!" he shouted as a swarm of wraith like creatures flew over our heads, their shrieks deafening. Without thinking, I pulled Etta to my chest, curling myself over her like a shield.

"Go!" I pushed her into the office. Owen slammed the door shut behind us.

"Professor! Professor Capra?" Cariss shouted. Silence met us as we skidded to a stop before his ancient door inlaid with gold scrollwork.

We halted at the threshold. The hairs on the back

of my neck stood on end as my werewolf senses tingled.

The door creaked open. Etta gasped.

"Professor Capra," Tatianna's whisper dropped into the heavy silence.

The professor stood in his doorway, his rotund belly stretching the gold buttons of his velveteen vest, his goat legs planted heavily on the floor. He gripped his cane. His whole body flickered. Like he was desperately hanging on to his corporeal form.

"The magic," The aged faun halted as his form shuddered in and out of visibility. "It is...taking us...old ones. Too much...magic...stored inside."

"What do we do?" The words sounded like my voice, though I wasn't sure I'd uttered them. Etta grasped my shaking forearm.

"You need...a unicorn." His body shivered violently and when it returned, he was completely see-through.

"Look...below..." He tapped his cane.

POOF!

With a wail that sent the group of us cowering, Professor Capra burst into a cloud of black and went screeching out the door, a phantom ghost himself.

"This is *so* bad," Tatianna whispered. Her eyes were fully enflamed, only just keeping her fire inside.

"A unicorn?" Cariss said.

Etta's hand was still on my arm. I clutched it.

"Nobody has seen a unicorn in a thousand years," Etta breathed.

We were screwed.

ETTA

Fennrick gripped my hand like it would keep him from drowning. Despite our heinous circumstances, it sent heat shooting to my middle. I *liked* the way his hand felt wrapped around mine. It gave me a fleeting feeling of security along with a wild rush of emotion. And then there was his smell. His mouth-watering scent. I knew it was his Alpha pheromones hard at work, but it was nearly enough to make me forget our dire situation. That and the fact that I'd wanted to be Fennerick's girl since I was thirteen, long before his Alpha genes kicked in.

"Where do we find a unicorn?" Owen asked, the tips of his pointed elf ears going as pale as the rest of his ashen skin. His question jerked me back to the present.

"What was it the professor said before he disappeared? 'Look below?' What does that mean?" Fenn asked the group.

"Look below," Cariss repeated, a crease forming between her eyebrows. "Below where?"

"Below, like below a bridge with the trolls?" Owen snorted.

"Below the ground?" Tatianna offered. She leaned into Owen, her inner fire going down to a simmer as he looped an arm around her shoulder.

"Below ground? Below ground where?" Cariss tapped her lip.

"What if he meant below the school?" I offered. The suggestion sounded ridiculous the moment it left my lips, and I felt my cheeks heat in response. Fenn looked at me.

"No. What if he *did* mean below the school. He tapped the floor right before he disappeared. Could there be a place *below* the school? We all know there are tunnels down there...but what if there's something...else?"

Cariss cocked her head to the side. "Well, the school is, what, a thousand years old?"

"No one has seen a unicorn in a thousand years," I murmured.

"Could that be a coincidence?" Fenn's fingers squeezed mine. A faraway look flashed through his eyes.

"Would the library still have original blueprints of the school?" he asked.

"Let's go look. We're not getting anywhere just standing in Professor's office," Tatianna said as she stalked towards the door.

The ancient Gothically arched hallways were eerily silent as we made our way to the library. The students racing around earlier were either gone or had hopefully made it to safety. Even the wraith-like creatures were gone. Erratically flickering bits of magic were the only noises as they hissed and popped in the top-most cracks and crevices of the arches.

The library doors were open, just like on any normal school day. The floor to ceiling bookshelves were crammed with everything from ancient scrolls to modern day paperbacks.

"In the resource room?" Cariss shrugged.

"Good a place as any to start," Fenn replied. My skin tingled as he touched my back to move me in that direction. I needed to get a grip.

Dust and age-old magic ticked my nose, and I clapped a hand over my mouth to catch my sneeze.

"Bless you," Fenn whispered, still close to my side.

"Thanks," I sniffled.

"Where do we start?" Tatianna asked as we broached the resource room. Tall scrolls and heavy ancient tomes scattered the large room.

"Time for the wolves to come out to play." Fenn nodded to Cariss and me

then wasted no time. He

jerked his arms backwards, taking his shirt off in that way only guys do. I'd seen him shirtless countless times over the years growing up in the same werewolf pack. But his abs were a lot nicer now than they had been a few years ago.

Cariss elbowed me and I blushed to the roots of my hair.

"Right. The older the document, the mustier it will smell," I stammered, fervently hoping Fenn didn't notice. Cariss and I quickly ducked behind a heavy-laden bookshelf and shifted to our fur.

I sneezed again as spangles of warped magic tickled my wolf's senses. Following Fenn's instructions, we quickly put our noses to work. It wasn't long before we'd unearthed a stack of ancient scrolls tucked neatly away in a forgotten box. Scents of stale magic and aged parchment for the win.

"Hurry up and shift back, guys," Tatianna said as she poured over the scroll.

"I think this might be it. Look," Owen said excitedly.

Within a minute, we were back in skin and taking in the prints.

"It's like a labyrinth." I shuddered.

"Roll the prints up. We'll take them with us." Fenn took charge. Owen carefully rolled the blueprints.

Minutes later the five of us stood facing a heavy iron-bound door at the end of a seemingly abandoned corridor deep in the belly of the Academy.

"I don't like this," Cariss whispered. I knew how she felt. Night had fallen. It was pitch black but for the occasional spatter of unhealthy magic and the glow of the one torch we'd been able to successfully light with fragmented strings of partially exhausted magic.

Fennrick reached for my hand. I didn't object.

"Tatianna, keep your flames close in case that thing goes out," Owen said.

"No problem with that," she replied, swallowing hard.

"I'm going in fur," Fenn said. "Carry my clothes?" he asked me. I swear a light blush stained his cheeks. I hoped he couldn't hear my heartrate pick up.

"Sure," I squeaked. He didn't need to explain that his wolf had better night vision and a better chance of defending us should it come to that.

Cariss opened the door.

A smell like wet death filtered up from the massive black hole before us. I shivered and Fenn's tail brushed against me.

"Let's go." Cariss' voice wavered.

Tatianna held the torch high. Fenn went in first.

The stones were damp and there was the occasional squelching noise that I refused to think too hard about. Deeper and deeper, we went into the ground. First through damp bricked arches, then into rough, hand-hewn stone passages.

"How old do you think this is down here?" Cariss whispered. I'd been wondering the same thing.

Fenn growled low in his throat, his ruff standing on end.

Wind whooshed up the rough corridor and sent my hair flying as a scream built in my throat.

A deep roar boomed up from the depths. Fenn planted himself in front of the group, his own deep warning echoing back and mixing with the echoes of the *thing* until it made my ears ache.

The torch flickered out and Tatianna screamed. Her eyes flashed once in the dark before a white-hot stream of lightening-like fire streaked from her eyes and illuminated the entire hallway.

A black apparition wavered in the dark shadows. My body froze, terror crawling over my skin like a hundred spiders.

"Light the torch, Tatianna," Owen commanded. "Don't char me in the process."

Breathlessly, we waited for the *thing*, listening, straining our senses. My hands gripped Fenn's clothes hard enough my knuckles cracked, and I wondered if I should shift to my fur, too.

Flames engulfed the torch, igniting frayed bits of magic as the fire burst onto the stone ceiling.

The apparition hadn't advanced. It wavered there on the outskirts of the torchlight.

Fenn growled low in his throat and scented the air. All I smelled was toasted magic and fear. Possibly my own.

"I don't think it's real." Owen whispered.

"You sure?" Tatianna said.

"If it were alive, I'm pretty sure your flame fest would have fried it. Look. I think it's just a magic illusion," Owen explained.

Fenn nudged me closer to Cariss with his tail, yipped at Owen, then stalked down the dark hallway.

"Be careful," I whispered.

I held my breath as Fennrick tracked down the hallway, his growls echoing off the stone walls. About halfway down the hall towards the floating black mass, his posture relaxed, and he trotted back to us.

He barked once and my shoulders relaxed.

"Not real then?" Owen confirmed. Fenn bobbed his head and met my eyes before jerking his head for us to move forward again. He brushed against my side as we went down the corridor, sending flutters into my middle while reassuring my jagged nerves.

The apparition disappeared the moment we stepped within a few feet of it. It was nothing but wisps of ancient magic, long forgotten by its creators.

We trudged on. After what felt like hours of wandering and multiple stops to consult the blueprints, we finally came to the deepest point marked on the prints. There was nowhere else to go. A solid door fitted with an iron latch stood between us and whatever waited on the other side.

Fenn nudged me and Cariss behind him again and nodded to Owen.

Grasping the doors as Tatianna's eyes flashed with ready flames, Owen pulled the latch. A loud *clink* echoed down the stone corridors. Goosebumps rippled down my skin.

The ancient door swung open.

Caked in dust, cobwebs, and strings of fluttering magic, the most majestic of all beasts stood solitarily in the middle of a tiny stone chamber.

A unicorn.

The golden horn was tightly wrapped with magic, though pieces of it hung in strips. Whole pieces of what appeared  to be magic-spun cloth were sagging from its white form like ripped pieces of a funeral shroud. Cobwebs stretched from the beard to the chest. Shiny golden hooves were dull and brassy with age.

"Oh," Cariss gasped.

The nostrils flared. My heart slammed into my throat. Fenn's tail pressed against my leg as his lips pulled back from his teeth.

Ever so slowly, with a noise like cracking plaster, the eye lids fluttered, breaking free of their ancient crusts.

The creature shrieked and shook the dust from its coat.

The noise echoed in my chest and sent me cowering on the ground. My hands clapped over my ears; eyes and ears both smarting from the bits of magic flung from the unicorn. All of us were huddled, in awe and fear, staring at the creature of legend before us.

"What has happened to the magic?" The unicorn's voice, rich like dark chocolate, smooth like velvet, and hard like diamonds, thundered in the tiny space.

We were too shocked to answer.

"What has happened to the magic?" the unicorn bellowed.

"A...a girl, a werewolf, fell onto Yggdrasil's roots." Cariss was the first to find her voice.

The unicorn snorted.

"We've no time to lose. Come."

The unicorn stamped his front hooves, the sound reverberating around us. In awe, we watched as the dirty hair and strings of magic fell away. The coat grew thick and shiny, the hooves and horn glowed with the inner magic of the unicorn.

"Wolf, you may change back. No harm shall befall you whilst in my company."

Fenn bobbed his head at the unicorn's words.

I gathered his clothes into a neater pile on the ground where I'd dropped them then nudged them towards him and turned. He quickly shift-ed back, and I let myself sag a little in relief as he took my hand once he was back in skin.

The trip back through the twisty, winding un-derground took a fraction of the time with the unicorn confidently leading the way.

I was bursting with questions, but I didn't think it would be appropriate to barrage a creature so rare that it had nearly faded into myth. It seemed too irreverent.

Instead, I clung to Fenn's hand, trying not to think how much I was going to miss it and *him* once our world was righted. Assuming it *could* be fixed.

The hall was pitch black and deathly quiet as we crept from the belly of the earth.

"You may extinguish the torch."

Tatianna did as the unicorn told her. With a toss of its mane, light emanated from the unicorn.

"Have you any mode of transport that will take you quicker to Yggdrasil? In my day we'd have to round up some wild gryphons and magic them or make the journey on foot."

"We've got a Jeep," Fenn offered.

"A Jeep. What manner of beast is this? Some new hybrid, perhaps?"

"It's…a mechanical beast." Fenn rubbed the back of his neck.

The unicorn snorted. "All this magic and they still tinker with mechanics." The front doors of the school loomed ahead in the shadows.

"Please, Sir, do you have a name?" Tatianna asked tentatively.

"I am Lazaren."

Tatianna quickly introduced each of us as we walked and exited the building. Wind and hail lashed around us as leaves and frazzled magic zinged and flew across the parking lot. Yet nothing touched us in the circle of Lazaren's glow.

"That thing is a Jeep?" Lazaren whickered in disdain as we reached the vehicle. "I shall meet you at Yggdrasil. See that you are not detained." With that, he broke into a gallop. Enormous white glossy wings edged in gold burst from the creature's back and he took flight, taking his inner light with him.

We were left again in darkness, suddenly caught in the uproar of the storm with his absence.

Yggdrasil was tempestuous, leaves stripped from its branches, magic gone but for a few bare tendrils stubbornly clinging to some odd twigs. Terror gripped me.

Lazaren stood beside the guardrail next to the glowing amber encasement where Lexie must have gone over. I bit the inside of my cheek, realizing I didn't know what had happened to make her topple over in the first place.

Lazaren asked my question in his next breath.

"What transpired here?"

Fenn rubbed the back of his neck again and refused to meet my gaze. "She tried to kiss me," he started. My hackles rose, even in my human skin. I had no formal claim on Fenn, but Lexie wasn't even a member of our pack.

"It wasn't Fennrick's fault," Cariss interjected. "I tried to stop her. I grabbed her arm."

Had Fenn *not* tried to stop Lexie?

"She jerked back and tripped."

"And I wasn't fast enough to stop her," Fenn interjected.

"And when she hit the roots, the world fell apart." Cariss shrugged, her misery clear. I squeezed her arm, and she gave me a grateful ghost of a smile.

Lazaren looked hard at each of us in the group. My skin tingled. Not in a bad way, but in an anticipatory sort of way.

Gingerly stepping over the guard rail, magic flared to life beneath his golden hooves as they touched Yggdrasil. It didn't spread, but illuminated Lazaren, and cast light back onto the pulsating amber glow over Lexie.

"You tried to take something that does not belong to you," the unicorn said over the quivering amber. I was close enough I could see Lexie's eyes widened, though the rest of her body stayed still. "I will let you out, but until the wrong has been righted, the magic will not be reversed." He glanced back at us. "No one touch the magic or the tree."

Raising up on his back legs, Lazaren cried into the air and brought his flashing hooves down. Yggdrasil's roots quivered. "Let her go. I am here now," the unicorn said to the ancient tree. Yggdrasil groaned.

I shivered as beads of frantic magic skittered over my skin. With a pointed look at me that dropped my stomach to my toes, Lazaren wrenched his horn through the crust of swirling amber. A noise like thunder booming over the ocean echoed around us.

Without meaning to, I gripped Fennrick's hand. His fingers squeezed tight around mine.

Gasping and spluttering, Lexie sat up.

"Lexie!" Cariss said in relief.

"Phoenix, seal the gap once she's up," Lazaren instructed.

Tatianna nodded and Owen reluctantly let her step closer towards the barrier.

The unicorn prodded his horn at Lexie, and in a show of great humility on his part, let her maneuver herself up using his mighty horn as leverage.

As soon as Lexie had cleared her magic cocoon, Tatianna let her eyes blaze. Chills tickled my arms as the flames danced in her eyes before they shot out in a stream of white-hot fire over the gap in the amber crust. It sealed together like it was welded with lava.

Storm clouds still thrashed overhead, and magic and lightning lit the sky as they clashed together. Sparks flew and shattered on the ground. Fenn tugged me closer so that my arm brushed against his side.

"I...I'm so sorry," Lexie whispered brokenly against the gale that whipped the leaves into little funnels around us.

Lazaren stared at Fenn solemnly. "T'was you who was wronged, Wolf. You must right it."

Fenn's face paled, and his throat bobbled as he swallowed. Slowly he turned to me. Lightening flashed and showed me his hazel eyes, full of questions and hope.

"Etta," he rasped. My heart sped up. "Lexie tried to take what's rightfully yours. I mean, mine to give, but only for you to take."

Understanding dawned and my lips parted in surprise. Alpha pheromones flooded the air around us and my heart pounded in exhilarated expectation.

"You want *me*?" I whispered.

"Yeah. I really, really do." He smiled, though uncertainty crept into his eyes.

Tingling rushed through me as *rightness* settled over me. His hand dropped mine and tentatively grazed my waist.

A wave of heat crashed through me, and my answering smile stretched my face.

"Yes." I breathed the word.

Fenn's eyebrows crinkled as his eyes turned serious. Wind whipped hair into my face, but before I could move it, he nudged it aside as his hand cupped my jaw. Tilting my face, his lips closed softly over mine.

Literal sparks exploded around us. We jerked apart, startled, and watched as magic whirled in the sky and came streaming, rushing, swirling back to Yggdrasil. Leaves reeled from the ground back into the leafy boughs. Sunlight broke through the black clouds and bathed the ground in iridescent sparkles that came up and flitted around us.

Tatianna laughed as some of the sparkles landed in her hair and lit it up like a halo. She let the flames rise in her eyes and let loose a stream of fire towards the rising sun, lighting a path straight over the top of Yggdrasil.

Fenn kissed the side of my head while we watched, but I turned and tugged his head back down for another, longer one.

He pulled me flush against him, his scent closing in around us. His smell slowly began to change, and I realized his hunt for the other half of his pair—for *me*—was over.

"Well done, children," Lazaren said. "You have saved your world, but if we do not return quickly to the school, without my stabilizing presence, so many different kinds of magic in one place will cause another explosion. I will not be able to save you should that happen."

We raced back to the Academy, magic swirling happily once more, though anxiety sat heavily with us. Lexie remained silent in the back seat. Lazaren again awaited us as we pulled into the parking lot and hopped out.

Relief was potent as I saw Professor Capra waiting at the double doors. He bowed low as Lazaren approached and we followed behind.

"Lazaren. Old friend. Thank you once again for your sacrifice." The old faun's horns were parallel to the ground as he used his cane to help him show his reverence.

"Capra." Lazaren inclined his head towards the professor.

"Children, follow me once more into the labyrinth."

We didn't dare question him, so we once more made the long trek into the darkness of the underside of the school. Lexie trailed uncomfortably behind. It wasn't as scary this time with Lazaren's glow and with Fenn's fingers laced with mine. I sighed in contentment.

We reached the tiny stone chamber once more, the door still standing open.

Lazaren stopped just outside the door.

"You will be the next generation of leaders of this place. Capra will not live forever. Remember my existence."

And with that, he went in and stood in exactly the same spot and the same position as when we found him.

With a twist of his head, my mouth fell open as strands of magic wound around his horn, funneling over his sleek body, coiling and weaving together in a magnificent tapestry of swirling, sparkling magic.

Once the magic had encased his full body, he turned his face to us. He gave us a sleepy wink with one drooping eyelid, then he went still.

I squeezed Fenn's hand.

Our world was safe once more.

A Feather & a Wink

AJ Skelly

A Feather & A Wink

"Would you move, you worthless bag of feathers!" I put my full weight behind the shove I give my gryphon, but it's no use.

He's rooted. He's staring. Strike that, he's pining. He's literally wiggling his feathery eyebrows...at *her*.

My forehead slumps against Griff's furry shoulder.

Heather Dewslip ambles towards the green, her regal gryphon following sedately on her leash like a good gryphon should. My head sinks farther against Griff's warm fur. His lion's tail flicks my back.

I've had the biggest crush on Heather for months, and it's mortifying. She's part fae; she can literally *see* emotion. Every emotion is a different color for her. She has to know my heart beats faster and my palms sweat every time she passes me. Who knows what color my embarrassed infatuation is? But to make matters worse, Griff also has a thing for her.

And he's not subtle.

He has never been the model gryphon. We're in the Gryphon Riders Training Course at Magik Prep Academy, but it's not going as well as I'd hoped. He can't keep his feathered head straight any more than I can once Heather comes on the premises.

"Assemble!"

I startle. I hadn't heard Professor Autun's goat feet in the soft grass of our landing green.

I sigh. "Okay, Griff. Let's try this again. Maybe you could show off for Heather instead of watching her the whole time and missing all our cues?" I pat his heavily tufted ear.

He growls low in his throat and ruffles his neck feathers. As I stroke his shoulder once more, he kneels down and lets me hop up onto his broad back. I settle my legs in front of his massive wings and grip tight with my knees. My hands clamp around his ear tufts so I can steer my huge beast. We tried a saddle and bridle early on but found that we prefer the natural way of riding together. I settle my weight and turn my attention back to the professor.

"Today, we're working on group maneuvers. You'll practice with one assigned partner and work on flying close brushes safely before we attempt moving as a larger group." Professor Autun pairs us off. I try not to fidget on Griff's back. His gaze is still stuck on Heather.

"Ryder and Heather."

A gasp freezes in my throat as Griff puffs his chest out and swishes his tail. He's thrilled. My stomach knots. Emotion surges through me, and I'm terrified it's being broadcast in neon colors above my head.

Heather sidles over on her gryphon, Sasha. "Um, I think your gryphon just winked at me."

"Yeah. Sorry about him." I swallow hard and pat him none-too-gently, reminding him to behave. "I think he has a crush on you." I want to swallow my tongue as soon as the words leave my mouth. Her face tints the lightest shade of pink.

"That's very flattering, Griff," she tells my beast with a sweet smile.

I gulp back my own emotions, desperately hoping they're not lighting up the sky like a flare.

"I'm still pretty new to this type of flying. Sasha and I haven't had a lot of practice with other riders. Can you walk me through it while we're in the air?" Heather shrugs apologetically.

"Sure. I mean, we've done some of this, but not a lot."

"I'm sure we'll figure it out." She gives me a sunny grin.

My heart lurches, and my cheeks heat. I heel Griff around into position and tug his ears to signal takeoff.

The wind rushes past my face, sweeping my anxiety and worry over my fluorescent emotions with it. For just a moment, I tip my head back and close my eyes, letting the euphoria of flying exhilarate me to my fingertips.

Sasha caws behind us and playfully rushes past us. Smiling, I nudge Griff and we take off after her.

We glide, urging our mounts close enough that their wings almost brush. Sasha is a little rocky, unsure of her movements in the rotation, but she soon seems to find her rhythm.

"It's glorious up here in the sky, isn't it?" Heather calls across a cloud.

I can't help my answering grin as I look at her. "Beautiful."

Someone shrieks behind us, and I crane my neck, trying to see.

"Dragon!"

"Dragon on the loose!"

"Oh, no!" I take a firmer clamp on Griff's ears. "Someone from the Dragon Apprenticeship Class must have lost their beast again. How does Sasha do with dragons?"

"Ryder!"

My head whips around as Heather screams. A panicked adolescent dragon is heading straight for her. Flames shoot from its nostrils, its ruby wings flailing as it tries to correct its terrified flight.

Sasha rears and screeches, frantically flapping her wings to get out of the way of the careening monster.

She's not fast enough.

"Griff, *go!*" I put my heels to his flanks and yank on his tufts. We shoot forward just as the dragon crashes into Sasha's chest.

Screeching and bellowing echo in the blue sky around us. The two great beasts go plummeting.

"Heather!"

She tumbles off Sasha's back with a yell as Sasha's tail tangles around the dragon's horns.

"Move, Griff!" I shove his tufts hard downward to steer him after Heather's falling form.

With a distressed screech of his own, Griff tucks his wings as I clench my legs, and we swoop.

Keeping my legs locked, I let go with my hands, trusting Griff to keep our trajectory.

Straining, I miss. Desperately I reach again.

"I gotcha!" I grip Heather's arms, hauling her over Griff's back, heart thundering in my chest.

"Ryder!" She gasps in relief as her hands lock around my middle. Griff rights himself and gracefully finishes his descent to the green.

"Are you all right?" I turn to her.

Heather blinks wide, purple eyes as she stares at me, still breathing hard. "Thanks to you." She studies me as her erratic breathing calms and my palms begin to sweat. "This is the first time your aura has been one color."

"What?"

"Your emotions—they're always so clouded, I can't ever tell what you're feeling. But right now, you're solid yellow. Relief." She smiles.

My heart accelerates.

"But now that there's a smidge of pink that I've been hoping I'd see..." A mischievous smile tips the corners of her mouth. "Would you like to go out sometime?"

A grin stretches across my face.

Griff will never let me hear the end of this.

Magik Prep Academy
Twist
of
Fate
AJ Skelly

TWIST OF FATE

This was it. Tonight was the night. Fate was on my side, I was sure of it. I was going to man up, be brave, and tell Qianna how I felt. I snagged a random piece of orange magic off the dresser and used it to help tie my cravat. My fingers trembled slightly.

I groaned as a scrubbed a hand down my face. "Because the annual All Hallows Eve Festival is a great time to declare your undying love. 'Oh, look, there's a severed hand dangling from a string of magic. Will you go out with me?' Flipping brilliant," I said to myself as I checked out my mop of light brown hair in the mirror that hung over my dresser in the dorm. My hair actually looked good today. Of course, it did. I'd be covering it up with my costume.

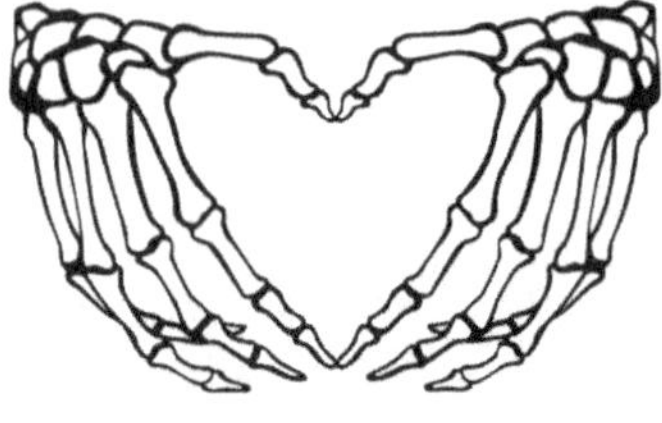

I rolled my eyes as my heart pounded. "No," I commanded my mirror self. "You are not going to chicken out. You are going to do this." I glared at myself for good measure, green eyes narrowing back at me. I'd been in love with my best friend for the past five years. That was five years too long to go without saying something.

And because I'd reached the point where keeping our platonic friendship was a form of torture in itself.

With a flick of my wrist, I donned the black cape and added the Victorian top hat. I squinted at myself in the mirror as I adjusted the fake mustache and half-mask covered in gears and a fake monocle. At least my lips were still available. Just in case Qianna wanted them...for any-thing.

I groaned and my internal magic slithered un-comfortably through my gut. My belly quivered with pent up nerves—anxiety both at the thought of her returning my feelings or rejecting them. It was a toss-up. But tonight, I was determined to take the risk. I needed it out in the open so it would stop festering inside me.

"Jamie," Tom, my suitemate, called down the hallway from the common room. He'd been playing lookout. His date was working the evening shift—they'd go to the festival lat-er. "Your friends are here!"

My heart thundered in my chest. It was time. Plan Expose My Heart To Qianna Step One: Make It Down The Hallway. I swirled my cape for good measure then swept down the re-modeled ancient stone corridor, nudging a few strands of magic away with the points of my pol-ished shoes.

"Have a good time, Jamie." Tom met me at the end of the hall, waggling his eyebrows. "Go get your girl," he whispered.

"Tom," I muttered, secretly pleased at his vote of confidence. I could only guess at how many conversations and laments he'd been forced to listen to about my unrequited love. They probably numbered in the hundreds at least. He winked, the velvety coating of his budding horns catching the torchlight. Still smiling, he trotted down the hallway, his goat hooves clacking against the stone floor. I felt the noise reverberating in my bones next to my rising anxiety. I resisted the urge to tug my sleeves down as I entered the common room.

And there she was. A Victorian steam punk teenage dream. Qianna stood there like an ethereal statue, her dark waves peeking out from a silly hat, a partial face mask like mine slipping back behind her pointed ears, and a deep purple dress that cinched in her tiny waist and poofed the rest of the way to the floor. I'd be lying if I said I wasn't enjoying the wide view of her collarbones and shoulders, too. Euphoria engulfed me—here she was. I'd dreamed about this night for weeks.

My dream came crashing down around my own pointed ears two seconds later when Andy Mitchells stepped through the front door dressed *exactly* like me—down to the fake monocle, black pants, and suit tails.

"You guys coming?" he called.

"Come on, Jamie! We're going to be late." Qianna grabbed my hand, sending shivers of sweet agonized torture up my arm, and dragged me toward the door. "Bye, Tom!" Qianna hollered as she shut the door to the dormitory behind us.

The night air was chilly, cooling my over-heated emotions. "I thought we were going just the two of us dressed all Victorian steam punk?" I said quietly

as we walked through the courtyard of the school to the Academy parking lot and Andy's waiting car. It'd taken Qianna two weeks to talk me into this madness, not that I'd tell her I was enjoying it, but I was steamed that Andy-the-popular was horning in on my exclusivity.

"I thought so, too, but I guess Andy overheard and thought it'd be cool." She shrugged a bare shoulder. "Someone posted about it on one of the social scroll feeds. A couple other girls from school and some their boyfriends decided to go steam punk, too. I guess we'll all be trying to channel history with our own magical flair." She smiled and her tiny dimple appeared on the left side of her mouth.

I resisted the urge to growl even as I was distracted by her dimple. I didn't care that other people were dressing similarly to us, I cared because Andy-the-jerk-face was my biggest competition for Qianna's affections. I knew he liked her. What I didn't know is whether Qianna liked him back. I hadn't been brave enough to ask her outright, though I'd seen her looking at him over-long a few times. I bit the inside of my cheek.

"It'll be fun, you'll see," Qianna said, her white teeth sparkling in the magicked light streaming down from the lampposts above us. Stars speckled the darkening sky.

"I hope you're right," I said. More than she knew. We reached the car.

"Here, Qianna. Your dress is huge. Why don't you sit in front so it doesn't get smashed."

"Oh, thanks, Andy. You sure?" Qianna said, oblivious to his ulterior motives. Since when had

Andy Mitchells ever been worried about a girl setting wrinkles on her skirt?

"You weren't worried about my skirt," Tekiesha, Qianna's best friend, hollered from the back seat as I slid in behind the passenger side and plopped next to her while Andy-the-chivalrous held the door for Qianna. Hard to get the door for the girl when you have to crawl back behind her seat to get to your own.

"Hey, Jamie," Tekiesha said, scooting over so I didn't mash her voluminous skirt.

"Hey, Kiesh. You look great," I said, trying to keep the jealous misery out of my voice. Her lips curved upward. The rest of her face was obscured by little gears and a few brightly colored feathers. It was a cool look and matched the deep orange of her dress. Her nose wrinkled.

"Wow, who's wearing the Kaboom cologne?" she asked.

"I am," I answered the same time Andy said, "Me."

"Guess that's why it's a little strong. Smells great, just a lot of it in the one car." Kiesha laughed.

Andy grunted and cracked the window.

It wasn't my favorite scent, but I knew Qianna liked it. Snakes writhed in my belly.

Kiesha's phone dinged. She gasped. "Qi, you will not believe this. Cora just texted me. There are at least seventeen other girls who did Victorian steam punk costumes after word got out that's what we were doing." Tekeisha was annoyed and snorted her irritation. I surreptitiously wiped my arm on the inside of my cape.

Qianna craned around in her seat as The Jerk drove us toward the fairgrounds a few miles from the Academy. "Are you kidding? Ugh. So much for being original. Oh well. I mean, I thought a few others might, but seventeen is kind of a lot."

Kiesha signed dramatically. "It's so hard being the best friend of a trendsetter." She tossed her hand over her masked face like she was fainting.

"See, I told you it wouldn't be so bad," Qianna said turning to me and squeezing my knee. My heart jumped painfully against my ribs. I tried to smile. "At least there will be other dudes in capes and hats." She smiled, her cheeks squishing into her mask.

My confidence withered. Not only would Andy-the-arrogant look just like me, who knew how many others would too? I had hoped this would be a special thing between just me and Qianna tonight. No such luck.

The fairgrounds were done up in typical Hallows Eve splendor—fake body parts dangling from low-hanging limbs, several well-placed fog machines, ghosts twitching in the breeze, magic spritzing and sparking dramatically. My mouth watered as a gust brought the scents of funnel cake, caramel apples, and roasted nuts in sugarberry glaze over to us.

"That smells amazing!" Qianna said as we stepped through the ticket booth and into the fair grounds.

"Let's split a funnel cake," Andy said. He grabbed Qianna's elbow, steering her towards the booth.

"He's so pushy," Kiesha said as we trailed.

I was too tied up in knots to say anything. If Andy leeched himself to Qianna all night, how was I ever going to confess my feelings to her?

"You're quiet tonight, Jamie. You okay?" Kiesha asked softly. Qianna laughed at something

Andy-the-hilarious said as he nudged her with his elbow. I swallowed.

"Yeah. Fine. Cravat is just a little tight." I wiggled a finger between the frothy silk and my skin and released a little magic to dry the nervous perspiration slicking my skin.

Kiesha raised an eyebrow. I glanced around, scanning the area, searching for my courage.

"Hey, there's hot chocolate over there." I took the opportunity. "Qianna," I called a little louder than I probably needed to, "let's grab drinks while Andy gets the funnel cakes," I said.

"Excellent idea. Back in a sec!" Qianna twirled, her skirt swinging behind her as she broke away from Andy-the-poacher  and tugged my fingers when I didn't move fast enough. I wanted to grab her hand, hang onto it for dear life, but my hands started to sweat, and

I didn't want to be gross, so I let her fingers slip through mine.

We got in line for hot chocolate, the colored lights and strings of neon magic reflecting off Qianna's white mask dotted in tiny gears. I cleared my throat.

"So, what do you want to do next?" I needed an opening. I needed to tell her. Just blurt it out.

"I want to walk around, see everything. Probably do the magicked house or the house of mirrors. Definitely want to do the haunted trail through the woods."

I grinned. "Well, we have to do that." It was our best-friend tradition. We did the haunted trail every year together. Every year we were scared witless and ran screaming and laughing like little girls.

She grinned and leaned her shoulder against mine. Now. I should tell her *now*.

"Qi, there's something I need to tell you." The words grated from my throat.

"What's up?" She turned at looked at me, her eyes shrouded in shadows through the eyeholes of her mask.

My mouth opened, but before I could force any more words out, the moment was ruined.

"Here's the funnel cake. It's as hot as Qianna," Andy said with a laugh.

Qianna giggled. I imagined her rolling her eyes, but instead she light fingered a piece and popped it in her mouth. Then she licked the remaining powdered sugar off her finger, and I went weak in the knees.

"Got just a little sugar left behind," Andy-the-snake said. He brushed it off with the back of his knuckle.

Qianna chuckled nervously and wiped her hand over her face. I wanted to puke.

"This is really good. Here, Jamie, have a piece." She thrust the plate at me, our fingers touching. Automatically I stuck a piece of piping hot funnel cake in my mouth and burned my tongue.

But it was delicious.

"Are you serious? Look, guys! Ms. Elwood—English teacher Ms. Elwood—is in the dunking booth!" Keisha said before shoving a fistful of cake in her mouth.

Andy grunted. "No way. She gave me a D on my last essay. I'm totally dunking her."

Sure, Andy. Ms. Elwood gave *you that D. Your performance had nothing to do with it. Idiot.* I rolled my eyes as we meandered to the line for the dunking booth so Andy-the-showoff could exhibit his aiming prowess. I tried to tell Qianna while Andy-the-flirt made a show of bringing his arm back and using a pitcher's stance to entertain the rest of those gathered around.

"Qianna," I rubbed the back of my neck. "About what I was going to mention earlier..."

"Sure, Jamie." She turned to face me. The fair lights glinted off the black waves of her hair and the sight of her throat and shoulders in her dress momentarily robbed me of words.

"Yes!" Andy hollered. Poor Ms. Elwood floundered in the tank as water sloshed over the sides. The Jerk did a ridiculous victory dance and pumped his arm in the air.

"I wonder if that will result in the next D for Andy," Qianna whispered conspiratorially. Regardless, the moment was sunk along with my English teacher.

We visited the face painting booth where Keisha got flames magidked up her arms. The rest of us watched. Andy clung to Qianna like a second skin. Mine seethed. After Keisha's flames were set and sparkling, we wandered the food vendors, sampling a few things.

"Is that frozen everflower juice?" Qianna asked around a mouthful of fresh donut.

"Wanna split one?" I asked. It wasn't uncommon for us to share food or drinks. And at the rate I was going, licking the spoon after her was likely to be the closest thing I came to tasting her lips tonight.

"Sure. You got the hot chocolate. I'll get the frozen everflower." She smiled at me—might as well have handed me the sun.

"Andy, look at this. Is this a two headed pig?"

"What?" Andy spun to look where Keisha pointed. Keisha winked at me behind Andy-the-gullible's back and tipped her head to the everflower stand. My cheeks flamed beneath my mask. Did Keisha know how I really felt about Qianna? Right then I didn't care. She was giving me an opportunity. I had to take it.

"Thanks for dressing up tonight, Jamie. I'm having a good time with it," Qianna said as we walked. I'd hand her the moon if she'd look at me again like she was now. Instead, I just grinned stupidly.

There was no line, so we got our cup of frozen everflower juice quickly.

"You want first bite?" she asked, extending the spoon.

"Nah, go ahead. I actually wanted," I cleared my throat, "wanted to tell you something."

She slipped a spoonful in her mouth but gave me her full attention.

"Something important," I reiterated. Where were all my carefully rehearsed words now? "I, well, for a long time I've been,"

"Qianna?" A new voice cut into my speech. I closed my eyes and only just kept myself from bowing my head in defeat.

"Doris? Wow," Qianna said as she took in Doris and a few other similarly dressed Victorian steam punk-clad classmates. She handed me the spoon and held out the iced everflower for me to take a bite.

Wow was right. Doris was a carbon copy of Qianna down to the placement of the gears on her blue half mask. Doris's mouth gaped.

"I feel like I owe you an apology. I could have sworn the guy in the costume shop said no one else had this specific costume," Doris said as she fidgeted with the corner of the black sash that went around the middle of her deep purple dress. She was as identical to Qianna as Andy was to me.

Qianna shrugged. "Maybe you got yours first? I don't know. I picked mine out in the store in the village but didn't ask if anyone else had it already. Anyway, it looks great on you."

A half smile turned Doris's lips. "You look better in it."

"All good. Hey, we were going to go over to the house of mirrors. You guys want to come?" Qianna motioned to the house of mirrors not far away.

A chorus of affirmation came from the group as Keisha and Andy-the-annoyed rejoined us.

Wonderful. More interruptions to my confession.

The house of mirrors was even more done up this year than it had been in years previous. The mirrors were taller, larger, and multiple fog machines and black lights laced with magic produced truly terrifying results in the mirrors. The whole herd of us jumbled inside the narrow corridors into the first of the large rooms, covered in mirrors. Where there had been about nine of us, there were now more like ninety with all the reflections. We trailed into the next room where not only were the fog machines and magicked black lights going, but there were also random bursts of strobe lights. It was horrendous. I was blinded, backed into, stepped on, and deafened by the shrieks of a few girls behind me.

It's also where I got separated from Qianna.

Half-blinded, cranky, and dejected, I searched the various rooms of the house of mirrors as best I could. It was impossible. They had to have gone on ahead of me. More people were filing in, and no one I came into the house with was in sight.

Finally, I stumbled my way into the last room of the house. I blinked through the fog and the daze the lingering lights left behind and moved to the side of the room to let my eyes adjust.

There.

Qianna stood all alone, her back to me, staring at her cloudy reflection through the fog. I swallowed on a suddenly dry mouth. This was it. No Andy-the-encroacher. No Keisha. No lines, no other interruptions. Slowly, I approached her. She didn't turn, though I knew she saw me in the reflection behind her.

"Hey," I said, my voice rusty. "I lost you guys."

Qianna smiled at me in the reflection.

"I, I need to tell you something. Something I've wanted to tell you for a long time."

Her smile stayed on her face, though my eyes dropped to the floor, unable to meet her gaze, even in the mirror, as I bared my soul. I'd better do it quick before something else could happen.

"I like you. More than like you."

She gasped and her hand flew to my arm.

"Just let me finish," I croaked, staring at her beautiful caramel-colored hand wrapped around my arm. "I think I'm in love with you," I whispered into the swirling fog. "I don't want to be just friends anymore. I want to be more than that with you." Hesitantly, I tipped my eyes up, meeting her shadowed ones behind the gears and glowing white of her mask.

"I had no idea," she whispered.

My whole body went rigid. My stomach plummeted; my feet rooted to the ground as horror coated the back of my throat.

She tore off her mask, and my fear was confirmed.

It wasn't Qianna behind the mask. I had just confessed my undying love *to Doris*. A good girl. But not the girl I wanted.

"Jamie, I, you're a nice guy, but I hardly know you. Sorry." Strobing magic caught the whites of her eyes, making them glow unnaturally.

"D, Doris. I," I coughed on the smoke and my embarrassment, "I'm so sorry." Then I took the coward's way out and fled the house of mirrors.

Quickly, I jogged down the gravel path that led back to the fairgrounds proper, totally mortified at what I'd unwittingly done. Right as I was about to turn to take myself back

toward the glowing neon

strips of magic, my eyes snagged on a top hat and a swish of purple skirt.

Halting, I stared in dread as Qianna reached up on tiptoe, her arms wrapped around Andy-the-winner's neck, and kissed him full on the mouth.

My stomach dropped to my toes as bile rose in the back of my throat. My heart cracked right down the middle.

Andy-the-thief slid his hands around her waist, one of them snaking up her back and tightening his hold on her. I was going to be sick. Rushing away before I could see anything else that would be forever imprinted on the back of my eyelids, I stumbled down the path.

At some point I found myself alone on the out-skirts of the fair near a trashcan that stank of stale hydra patties and kelp sauce. Sinking onto the bench, I let my head fall defeated into my hands. I ripped the stupid mask, mustache, and hat off then yanked my hands through my hair. I wanted to cry. Sob like a baby. My heart would never be the same again. There would always be a hollow place inside my chest now—the place Qianna was supposed to fill.

What was I supposed to do now? Act like it never happened? Tell her I saw her kiss my arch nemesis? Ask her to choose me instead? Questions and emotions swirled around inside me like a tornado.

I was so lost in my own turmoil of thoughts that it barely registered when someone sat down on the bench beside me.

"Hey," Qianna said softly. My head jerked up and I stared at her. She'd taken her mask and tiny hat off, revealing her face. She fiddled with a snippet of green magic, twisting it to smithereens. She looked miserable.

Miserable enough that it momentarily superseded my own quagmire of emotions.

"What's wrong?" I asked. If Andy...

She glanced at me. "I could ask you the same thing. You look terrible." She let the magic flutter to the ground and leaned her elbow on the back of the bench then scooted so she faced me, propping her chin on her hand. She sighed and looked away over the bright lights of the Hallows Eve festival.

"You first." I swallowed hard.

"I did something stupid," she confessed.

Yeah, ya did! my brain shouted. But it was Qianna. My entire life, all I'd wanted was to make her feel loved, protected, and in this case, less miserable.

"Yeah, well, I confessed my undying love and was turned down flat." The words tumbled out.

She snorted in surprise. "You did?"

"Yep. It was epically awful."

She sighed again. "I didn't know you liked anyone like that." She bit her lip. We were silent a moment. I couldn't bring myself to tell her the truth in the face of her shared lip-lock with Andy-the-vile. "That *is* awful," she continued. "About as awful as kissing the wrong person," she admitted.

I straightened on the bench. My heart pounded. "You didn't mean to kiss Andy?" My voice was breathless.

Qianna groaned, her face scrunching in embarrassment. "How do you know about that? It only happened fifteen minutes ago."

Heat crawled up my neck. "I saw you kiss him. After we got separated and I finally got out of the house of mirrors."

She waved her free hand helplessly in the air, her mouth moving as if searching for the right words. "I thought he was you," she finally blurted.

We were still a full minute as her words sunk in.

"You thought Andy was me? You were trying to kiss *me*?"

"We all got separated in the house of mirrors. Andy grabbed my hand and started leading me out the back. I thought he was you. He looked like you, he smelled like you, I was still seeing black dots from the strobe magic. Then when we were alone—I seized the moment and decided to be impulsive." She bit her lip again before looking me in the eye. "Jamie, we've known each other all our lives. We've been best friends since we were two. You've always been a part of my life. I *want* you to always be a part of my life. But somewhere along the way, I fell into wanting *more* with you. You get me like no one else. Honestly, I don't ever want anyone else to know all the things you know about me." She sighed heavily. "And now it's too late, because you like someone else."

I cracked a grin as my heart began pumping hope to all my extremities.

"So there you have my story of woe. Who are you in love with?" Her words came out bitter at the end. It filled me with unquenchable glee. She was jealous of my ignorant blunder.

"I'm in love with *you*." The words slipped out. "But I thought Doris was you inside the house of mirrors. I told her everything I've been trying to tell you all night."

Slowly, a hesitant smile slid over Qianna's lips.

"Lucky for me, she has terrible taste in men," I teased.

Her smile grew.

"Does this mean it's okay to kiss *you* now?" One slim eyebrow arched and sent my pulse skyrocketing.

A bark of laughter escaped my throat. "I've only been thinking about it for five years."

Still, she hesitated. "What an ironic twist of fate."

"I'm all for tempting fate tonight. Come here."

And she did."I'm in love with *you*." The words slipped out. "But I thought Doris was you inside the house of mirrors. I told her everything I've been trying to tell you all night."

Slowly, a hesitant smile slid over Qianna's lips.

"Lucky for me, she has terrible taste in men," I teased.

Her smile grew.

"Does this mean it's okay to kiss *you* now?" One slim eyebrow arched and sent my pulse skyrocketing.

A bark of laughter escaped my throat. "I've only been thinking about it for five years."

Still, she hesitated. "What an ironic twist of fate."

"I'm all for tempting fate tonight. Come here." And she did.

Selkie Skin Deep

AJ Skelly

SELKIE SKIN DEEP

I sat at the water's edge, afraid to get in, but longing for the cool brush of the water against my fur. As it was, I sat hunched on a rock beside the pool in my human skin, legs dangling in the shallows, stroking the worn pelt that had been handed down to me from generations past.

It should have been an honor to receive a sealskin from my forebears. And it was. I treasured the ability to shift into a seal when it covered me...but I was also ashamed of the sealskin.

My fingers traced a hole in the hide, patched with the skin from another seal. One a brown pelt, one spotted, the mending noticeable. Letting my eyes linger, I noted the places where the fur had all but been rubbed away. Thick pink scars roped over the side of one flipper and traced down the side. Holes left from fisherman's hooks punctured three places in the back, again patched with mismatched skin beneath.

A loud splash sounded to my left and a few errant droplets landed on my thigh. A group of girls splashed about, laughing and clapping their flippers at each other, swirling around each other playing Marco Polo in the deep end of the pool.

I'd wanted to come to Magik Prep since I was a girl, and my extended family all pitched in so I could achieve my dream. But doing so meant I used the sealskin that had been in my family for generations, rather than getting a new one of my own. I hadn't minded until I got to Magik Prep and started mingling with the rest of the selkies. Most of the girls were older, prettier, more confident, and had shining sleek skins that had shame burning in my gut when I looked at my own. How could I ever compare to them?

Seeing a filament of purple magic floating to the side of the ledge, as surreptitiously as I could, I snatched it and tried to weave it around the base of the scar puckering beneath the right flipper, trying to minimize it. It did no good. Selkies possessed their own magic, and while we could make our own and use it to transform our human bodies into the glossy bodies of the seals once we put on our pelts, something about our magic repelled it from other sources.

Sighing in frustration, I flung the useless piece of magic to the side.

Ripples danced around my ankles, and I turned my eyes to the water once more. My chest tightened as Janna's black seal head broke the water.

Janna was a senior, and so self-assured that I wilted in her mere presence. I simultaneously wanted to *be* her and wanted to curl up into a ball and hide my skin away from her. Her pelt was the glossiest, the shiniest, the most beautiful sealskin I'd ever seen.

Much to my surprise, she launched herself up out of the water, perching next to me, and let the top half of her sealskin fall away, revealing her wet ginger hair and freckled face. She held the skin about her chest with her arms, letting her foot flippers laze in the water, half human, and half seal.

"Hiya, Ellie. Not getting in the water today?"

I gulped and shook my head.

She cocked her head to the side, studying me. "Why not? Water's great. They fixed the filtration system last week you know. No more algae to clean off the pelts once we're done swimming." She grinned, giving me an excuse.

I cleared my throat. "I, I guess I just don't feel like it today," I said softly.

"Nonsense. Every selkie longs to be one with the water."

She was right. I ached to be in the water but lacked the courage to put myself on full display among all the perfect sealskins the other girls sported.

I shrugged, unsure what else to say.

"You know, my family would never dare let me out to the shallows with a sealskin as full of family history as yours is. What an honor to carry such a legacy. Your family must trust you and love you a lot."

I blinked at her words as a curl of heat bloomed inside me.

"Really?"

Janna nodded. "Really."

We sat in silence a moment longer as I turned her words over.

"I could be wrong in thinking this, and feel free to tell me if I am, but there is no reason you should be ashamed of your pelt. It's perfectly functional. You shift into a seal just as much as the rest of us. It's not the skin that makes the magic. That's in here." She tapped my chest and smiled. "Your insides make the magic. *You* are what's special. Not the skin. Your pelt is merely the tool you use. It's more important to be pretty on the inside than pretty on the outside. Without the magic inside, your pelt is just a piece of dead fur. The person behind it gives it life. Worry about the insides, and your outsides will shine just as beautifully."

With another smile, she tugged her pelt back over her face and disappeared once more beneath the waves to join the others.

I stilled on my rock, turning her words over and over in my mind.

Little pin pricks of magic coiled up inside me, tingling from my chest to my fingers. I stroked the sealskin in my lap, seeing it with new eyes. My family *did* love me. They *did* trust me. They wanted the best for me. That's why I was here.

They trusted me to be prettier on the inside than this pelt was on my outside.

Janna was right.

The insides were the things that counted most.

Glancing at the other girls in their sleek skins playing the deep, my fledgling confidence faltered. Screwing up my courage, I swallowed and let my sealskin encase me.

Jumping from my rock, the cool water embraced me, rushing over my fur, the patched spots disappearing, the ropy scar nonexistent as I glided through the water. They no longer mattered. They did not hinder my movements, they did not stop me from turning, tumbling, shooting through the water.

Maybe by worrying so much about the outsides, I'd missed the whole point of being a selkie. We *did*make our own magic.

I wanted mine to be beautiful.

"A refreshing take on magic school, teens with powers, and opposites attracting."
-MORGAN L. BUSSE, bestselling and award-winning author
of the *Ravenwood Saga* and *Skyworld* series
OF
FLAME &
FROST
AJ Skelly

EXCERPT FOR OF FLAME & FROST

ASPEN

Shadows lengthened in the darkening night, dancing and writhing with the bodies on the island.

"Come on, Aspen," Kasin said, tugging my hand. His cool blue eyes twinkled down at me as his perfect lips curved in a winning smile.

My knees went weak as the full force of that smile turned on me.

"I want to show you something." His lips tickled my pointed ear as he whispered. His hand snaked around the small of my back, guiding me down the path, away from the bonfire and the groups of dancing teenagers.

"Aspen, come dance with us!" one of the nymph girls called from a circle of twirling students. Her lithe, nearly translucent form swayed to the music. Curls of magic amplified the noise, setting the beat thumping in my chest. Kasin squeezed my hand as my heart picked up another notch. Parties on the island were common on the weekends. We needed a break from boarding school every now and then. But this was the first one I'd ever been to with Kasin.

"Maybe later," I called with a wave of my hand. The nymph winked at me, fluttering her long fingers.

"Kasin! They're setting up a game of catch the pixie! We had a freshman pixie volunteer! We can't let that go," an elf with ears pierced five times called.

"You can catch him on your own," Kasin called back with a grin.

"What? You're missing out!"

"Not this time," Kasin said softly to me as he tugged me deeper into the shadows surrounding several of the old buildings that dotted the island in the middle of the Chasm.

This was my first date with Kasin. We were both at the height of popularity at Magik Prep Academy and made quite the couple. Tongues had started wagging and gossip trembled down the magic strings the second we stepped foot on the Island together for tonight's party. I secretly hoped he had a romantic picnic set up in one of the buildings—a midnight snack just for the two of us. Frost tingled at the ends of my fingertips at the thought.

Kasin tugged an age-worn door open, lightly pushing me inside.

"What did you want to show me?" I asked as the door shut behind him, plunging us into darkness.

I could feel the heat coming off him as he stepped into my space. "This," he whispered as his lips covered mine.

Oh.

Part of me was disappointed that Kasin just wanted to make out. Not that I didn't enjoy being kissed, but I had hoped for a little more romance. For several minutes, his lips moved against mine, his arms holding me close.

Then, almost like a switch had flipped, his hands gripped me harder, sending my pulse spiking. Pushing against me with his hips, he backed me up until my back hit the rough wooden wall. His lips were hard, insistent. His hands found my hips, squeezing, dipping lower. I was not enjoying this anymore.

"Kasin," I dragged my lips away from the onslaught of his, trying to push him away. "Stop. I'm done."

"No, you're not. You've been flirting with me for weeks. All night you've been staring at me with those eyes. You've been telling me you want-ed this since the second we stepped foot on the Chasm bridge," he growled the words, pushing harder against me, his hands slipping up the sides of my shirt.

Ice crackled in my chest as fury radiated cold to my fingertips.

"I said *no*."

I grabbed his wrist, but he shook me off, the bulk of his body pinning me to the wall. Anger and fear twisted maliciously in my gut. Squirm-ing, I pushed against him. I might as well have been a sprite trying to take down an ogre.

"I know you want this. You're going to give me what you've been teasing." Lust practically leaked out of his pores as my heart galloped into my throat. This was bad. *Really bad.*

Black pin pricks dotted the outside of my vision as he rammed his shoulder into my solar plexus, keeping me from escaping as he undid the fly of his jeans.

Frost crept over my pillow, over the edge of my comforter. My heart pounded. My legs tried to run—run away—but I was stuck fast. He loomed over me. Terror and anger clouded my vision and the frost flowing from my fingers became ice. His hand swept towards me with fingers outstretched like claws.

I woke panting, heart drumming. A fine layer of ice crystals covered my blanket under my fingertips. A dream. It was only a dream. A dream wreathed in memory. Memory of what was—and what could have been.

Kasin was a boil on the backside of a pookah.

Blinking blearily, I rubbed the corners of my eyes. Squinting at the dial on my bedside table, I resisted the urge to groan, and forced my legs over the edge of my bed. The cold stone floor didn't bother me in the least, but I missed the warmth of my covers. Just because I was a frost fairy didn't mean I didn't like the heat. Shaking my head, I tried to leave the last vestiges of the memory-dream behind.

Trudging down the dormitory corridor to the communal bathroom, I paused as voices echoed into the ancient stone hallway. Knowing I probably shouldn't, I snagged a little piece of bright-colored magic that hovered near me, bending it to amplify what the girls were saying. Right as I finished contorting it, a shower turned on and I rolled my eyes. Flicking the magic away, I shuffled into the bathroom.

Tall and gorgeous, Tawny Evrel, and her side kick, short squatty Arietta Gowan, looked at me in the reflection of the mirror. The two biggest gossips at Magik Preparatory Academy. Arietta tittered and my stomach dropped to my toes.

"Honey, if you were that nervous, you could have asked me for some tips. I would have gladly shared." Tawny winked at me, though the gesture lacked kindness.

My white-blonde eyebrow rose. "Um, thanks," I said before ignoring them, swallowing hard, and heading to an empty shower stall. Arietta giggled behind her hand and that niggling finger of concern wiggled in my middle.

The refectory hushed as I came through the doors. The weight of the stares suddenly directed at me sat on my shoulders like a giant's hand pressing me into the earth. My fingers twitched as frost began forming on the underside of my tray without my permission. Why was everyone staring at me? My heart picked up, my pulse growing painfully pronounced.

Whispers began circulating like dragonfire, spreading from one table to the next.

Ice Queen, the whispers said.

Frost morphed into little chips of ice. My tray groaned. The whispers weren't referring to my ability to create ice on demand. My stomach plunged to my toes as I forced my chin into the air.

I turned to my regular table where my circle of friends sat, a collection of fae and a few other species. Before I could sit, Laara gave me a look of pity that made my toes curl.

"What?" I snapped irritably. I had no idea what everyone thought they knew about me. But as dread crept up my spine, I was willing to bet a season's snowfall that it had to do with Kasin Geethon. That smarmy toad.

"It's okay. We all know," Laara said, her eyes holding pity and a hint of embarrassment that bordered on predatory.

"Know what?" I ground out. My fingers bit into the shards of ice coating the underside of my tray.

"What happened at the party Saturday night," she whispered. Her eyes held the sort of wild delight that let me know whatever the grapevine said was salacious, juicy, and scandalous. And undoubtedly not the truth. My eyes narrowed as frost crept up the sides of my tray.

"What did Kasin say?" I asked through clenched teeth.

"Everyone is nervous their first time." Laara's saccharine voice grated my skin like sandpaper.

Anger boiled inside me, and I knew I needed to get outside where I could safely vent the ice that was going to blast out my fingers if I didn't release some tension *soon*.

I dropped my tray of untouched food onto the table. It cracked in half on impact. Turning on my heel, I stormed back out the doors. Snickers and a cat call followed me until the heavy oak door swooshed shut behind me.

Once I was in the courtyard, blessedly devoid of other students, I dug my fingers into the soft grass and let my frustration flow out of my fingers. Little raised bumps fractured away from my hands as ice displaced the dirt, leaving a long shaft of frozen frustration burrowing into the ground.

I straightened from my crouch and watched as Arietta crossed the far side of the lawn. My fingers curled into tight fists as her short legs clipped across the grass towards another girl exiting the refectory. Arietta's eyes were fairly sparking with a sort of fevered glow as she not so surreptitiously jerked her head towards me.

With a single flick of my wrist, I brought a cold wind whistling down from the eves and brought her hushed words to my ears.

"Yes, that's her. Aspen Frost. Kasin said she was so nervous after he kissed her that she literally froze her own thighs shut. Can you imagine? How humiliating! And after she's been leading Kasin on for weeks!"

Rage consumed me as a shower of snowflakes blanketed the roof.

COLE

The girls stared as I trudged down the stone hallway beneath the gothic-styled arches where strings of magic floated. All fire-drakes were alluring in their human form, though my mother's phoenix blood made me taller and slenderer than most. I gulped and made sure my mask of indifference was firmly in place. My hands clenched into fists inside the pockets of my magic-lined pants. I willed the flames that licked under my skin to settle. Anxiety still rippled up my spine. Blinking, I hoped my inner fire wasn't showing in my eyes.

The office was at the center of the building and it took half an age to get there. All the while, the stares of students burned into my back like hot irons. I hated being the new kid. But Magik Prep was my last chance. I'd been to three other lesser schools closer to home. To no avail. Magik Prep was supposed to be the best. If I couldn't learn how to control my fire here, then I'd be dangerous and alone the rest of my life. And that thought set my teeth on edge and my heart plummeting to my toes.

Maybe a monster like me deserved to live in isolation.

It didn't matter. At least, that's what I told myself as I put another brick in the wall around my heart. My walls were my defense. With an arrogant tilt of my chin, I tossed my black hair out of my eyes and opened the door to the office, careful not to touch the brass handle long enough it overheated.

"Good morning," a cheerfully plump woman greeted me. Tiny little horns poked through her curly hair. Her face was a veneer of heavy-handed makeup, but her eyes were genuine enough. She got up from behind her desk and tromped over to me on little goat feet.

"Here, dear, come right through here. You must be Cole? Cole Raiden?" She extended her arm to usher me in but was careful to keep her distance. At least there was no fear in her eyes. Yet.

I nodded and walked where she indicated.

"We'll just get you settled. I'm Ms. Pennywiggle."

I stifled a snort. Pennywiggle? She ignored my ill manners and rifled through a folder on a desk.

"There now. I've got your schedule here and a map of the school."

She handed the papers out to me. I stared at them.

"Don't you want to take them?"

My face flushed and fire raged through me, hot and uncontrolled.

"I can't," I grunted.

"Oh." Her eyes widened. "*Oh.*" She tapped her lip with a red manicured nail. "What did you do at your last school?"

I swallowed down as much shame as I could. "If you could lay them out on the desk, I'll look at them there."

She looked at me uncertainly but did as I asked. I smothered a sigh. I'd taught myself to memorize quickly years ago. I had to do something since flammable things turned to ash in my hands.

I studied my schedule then the layout of the school. Once I knew I had it down I nodded to Ms. Pennywiggle.

Orange light zinged down the office ceiling making me flinch.

"Don't worry about that, dear. It's just the magic. It's been laying around for centuries. We use it as we need it. The orange flash means ten increments until class starts. Do you want me to get an office aide to help you to your first class?"

No. No, I really did not want an office aide showing me to first period.

"I'll be fine," I said brusquely.

I shouldered my backpack, also woven with magic so it wouldn't catch fire every time I touched it, and slouched through the doors.

Careful to avoid contact with anyone, I moved down the hallway with serpentine grace and an arrogant smirk on my face that never failed to attract the girls and annoy the guys. I hoped my black clothes and equally dark expression would act as deterrent enough for people to leave me alone.

I was a powder keg waiting for the tiniest spark. That's all it would take for me to raze this place to the ground.

THE AUTHOR

AJ Skelly is an author, reader, and lover of all things fantasy, medieval, and fairy-tale-romance. And werewolves. She has a serious soft spot for them. As an avid life-long reader and a former high school English teacher, she's always been fascinated with the written word. She lives with her husband, children, and many imaginary friends who often find their way into her stories. They all drink copious amounts of tea together and stay up reading far later than they should.

You can read more of her short stories at www .ajskelly.com.

THE PUBLISHER

Find other Quill & Flame titles at www.quilland-flame.com or

@quill.and.flame.publishers on Instagram.

Stay tuned for more short stories as well as feature releases from Quill & Flame Publishing House.

Join Quill & Flame Book Tours by emailing quillandflamepublishinghouse@gmail.com.

OTHER QUILL & FLAME BOOKS

Stay tuned for more books releasing with Quill & Flame in 2023!

Heartmender by V. Romas Burton (2022)

Heartbreaker by V. Romas Burton (2022)

Heartrender by V. Romas Burton (2022)

Wishes by Brittany Eden (2022)

Making Magik by AJ Skelly

Fortified by V. Romas Burton

Of Flame & Frost by AJ Skelly

By Light & Love by Anna Augustine

R.E.M. by Ashley Schaller

Tide & Scales Anthology

Hearts by Brittany Eden

By Blade & Blood by Anna Augustine

Heart of the Sea by Moriah Chavis

Shadowcast by Crystal D. Grant

Lost Shift by AJ Skelly

Unleashed by Amber Kirkpatrick

Magic and Mistletoe Anthology

Magik Prep Academy